COLT IN THE CAVE

Mandy moved forward into the pitch-blackness. As the silence deepened, she suddenly became aware of a presence. Something strong and powerful was surrounding her and filled the dark void ahead. Was someone else in the tunnel with them?

She stared hard into the darkness beyond but could see nothing. She looked over her shoulder and the beam from her headlamp lit up only James's face. Mandy shone the lamp all around her, but it illuminated only the emptiness in the tunnel. Yet, somehow, she couldn't shake off the feeling that they were not alone. A shiver trickled down her spine.

"There's someone here with us," she whispered to James.

Read more spooky Animal Ark™ Hauntings tales

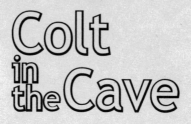

Colt in the Cave

Ben M. Baglio

Illustrations by Ann Baum

Cover illustration by
John Butler

AN
APPLE
PAPERBACK

SCHOLASTIC INC.

New York Toronto London Auckland Sydney
Mexico City New Delhi Hong Kong Buenos Aires

No part of this publication may be reproduced in whole or in part, or stored in a retrieval system, or transmitted in any form or by any means, electronic, mechanical, photocopying, recording, or otherwise, without written permission of the publisher. For information regarding permission, write to Working Partners Limited, 1 Albion Place, London W6 0QT, United Kingdom.

ISBN 0-439-34413-1

All rights reserved. Published by Scholastic Inc., 555 Broadway, New York, NY 10012, by arrangement with Working Partners Limited. ANIMAL ARK is a trademark of Working Partners Limited. SCHOLASTIC, APPLE PAPERBACKS, and associated logos are trademarks and/or registered trademarks of Scholastic Inc.

12 11 10 9 8 7   3 4 5 6 7/0

Printed in the U.S.A.   40

First Scholastic printing, January 2002

Special thanks to Andrea Abbott
Thanks also to C. J. Hall,
B.Vet.Med., M.R.C.V.S., for reviewing
the veterinary information contained in this book.

Where animals come first

One

"We're here!" Mandy Hope exclaimed to her best friend, James Hunter, as the bus turned off the main road and drove along a narrow, unpaved one.

A buzz of excitement erupted among Mandy's and James's classmates, who craned their necks trying to catch a first glimpse of the coal mine ahead. Mandy stood up, hoping to spot the mine before James did, but all she could see in the surrounding meadows were horses and cattle grazing peacefully in the soft, autumn sunshine. Two black Shetland ponies lifted their heads and stared inquisitively at the bus as it bumped along the dirt road.

"Aren't they gorgeous!" Mandy sighed.

James nodded. "I suppose if they'd been alive when the mine was working, they wouldn't be enjoying the sunshine — they'd have been down in the mine instead."

"I guess so," said Mandy, frowning solemnly.

"Hey, look!" cried James. He stood up to get a better view of the road ahead. "I think I can see the mine." He hurriedly began to take his camera out of its case.

Mandy followed James's gaze. An ugly black mound had appeared a few hundred yards ahead. It looked just like the pictures that Mandy had seen in books on coal mining.

The bus passed through an arched gate with a wrought iron sign that read "Amberton Mining Museum."

"This is going to be great!" declared James, taking a photograph of the sprawling mine buildings as the bus came to a stop in the gravel parking lot. "I can't wait to go underground!"

Mandy smiled. Ever since they'd learned that their two classes were visiting the mine, James had spoken of little else.

"Did you know," said James, "that about a century ago people our age used to have to work in the mine?" He grimaced. "I wonder what that was like." He stepped into the aisle of the bus, joining the throng of class-mates eager to start the tour.

"Didn't they go to school?" Mandy couldn't imagine having to work for a living yet. She squeezed into the aisle behind James.

"I don't think so," he answered. "Mrs. Black said that mining was a family tradition in those days. I would've looked up something about it on the Internet last night, but Dad's still having trouble getting the computer con-nected," he added glumly.

For months, James had been asking his dad if they could get onto the Internet. Finally, only a few days be-fore, he had called Mandy excitedly to tell her that Mr. Hunter had finally given in. However, something was wrong with the equipment and, meanwhile, James was having to wait patiently for the problem to be worked out.

Everyone piled out of the bus, then crowded around as Ms. Potter, Mandy's teacher, gave some last-minute instructions. "Before we start the tour," she announced, "I want to remind you about your projects. Remember, you're each to choose a specific aspect of coal mining. Take as many notes as you can on anything you learn about your chosen subject. If you haven't thought of a topic yet, don't worry. I'm sure something will interest you while we're here."

Mandy had chosen her topic a long time ago. When Ms. Potter first mentioned the project, Mandy knew immediately what she was going to research — pit ponies, the small but strong horses that had once worked down in the mines. Mandy loved all animals and was always eager to learn as much as she could about them. When she grew up, she was going to be a vet, just like her parents, Adam and Emily Hope. Their veterinary practice was called Animal Ark and was attached to their home in the Yorkshire section of Welford.

Mandy had already found a lot of information about pit ponies in some of her many animal books. She now knew that the ponies used in the pits were mainly Shetlands or Welsh mountain ponies. The poor creatures had to pull tubs heavily laden with coal from the coal beds to the elevator shaft, which was often quite a distance. But she was hoping to learn much more about the tough little horses at the mining museum.

The two teachers led the group to a redbrick building. Next to it was a tall steel structure with what looked like a big wheel at the top.

"That must be the winding gear," Ms. Potter told them. "It operates the elevator that goes underground."

"I hope it's strong," murmured someone at the back of the crowd. Some of the classmates giggled at the comment while others nodded in agreement.

A young woman dressed in a stylish black suit came out of the brick building to greet them. "Hello, everyone," she said with a friendly smile. "You must be the group from Walton Moor School. I'm Lisa Edwards and I'll be looking after you above ground. Before we start the tour, I'll just fill you in on some procedures. But first, have all your parents signed the waivers?"

Ms. Potter took out a thick wad of papers from her briefcase. "Here they are," she said, handing the forms to Lisa.

Mandy had read through the form with her parents the night before. It stated that the museum could not be held responsible for any accidents or injuries occurring on their property.

"Just a formality," her dad had said, as he signed on the dotted line. "I'm sure they'll look after you all."

"Thanks," said Lisa, taking the forms. "Now, because there are a lot of you, we'll divide you into teams. Some of you may not want to go down the shaft, so you can form one group, which I will take around. Those who *do* want to go underground will make up two more groups, each headed by a teacher."

The big group quickly split up and Mandy and James found themselves on Ms. Potter's team.

Lisa then explained that the mine was very old but it had closed down only fifteen years ago. "That means you'll see a lot of antique tools as well as more modern equipment. The heavy machinery and computer systems once used are in the exhibition hall down that hall," she said, pointing to her left.

"Are you going to do your project on the computer system?" Mandy whispered to James.

"No. I'm a little frustrated with computers at the moment," James said with a grin. Then he added more seriously, "I think I'm going to look at the tunnel system instead."

Lisa continued, "Some of you might be interested in visiting the blacksmith's yard next to the exhibition hall — you can learn a lot about the ponies that used to work here."

Mandy nudged James. "That's the part I'm looking forward to."

"Now, let's decide who's doing the underground tour first," said Lisa.

Mrs. Black tossed a coin. "Heads!" she announced.

"Oh, good!" said James. "That's us!"

Lisa then explained what would happen when it was time for the underground tour. "The trip down the shaft starts in fifteen minutes. A bell will warn you to make your way to the elevator in a few minutes' time. In the meantime, feel free to have a look around."

Mandy looked at her watch. "Let's go to the pony exhibit," she suggested to James.

"Okay," said James. "But listen for the bell. We don't want to miss the elevator."

They hurried through the big hall and out into a courtyard where some enormous machines were on display. James paused as they came to a massive piece of equipment. "It's a continuous mining machine," he read from the plaque. "It says here that this was one of the machines that replaced ponies in the mines."

Mandy was happy to hear this, but it also made her think of something else. "When you see how huge this machine is, it makes you realize just how hard the ponies had to work," she said somberly.

At the far end of the courtyard was a pair of strong wooden doors with a sign that said BLACKSMITH'S YARD. The two friends pushed open the doors and entered the deserted cobblestone yard.

Instantly, Mandy felt as if she'd been transported back to another time. The place was steeped in history. Everywhere there were signs of the ponies that had once passed through on their way to their underground lives. Harnesses hung from hooks on the rough brick walls and special head-protection devices were piled on shelves at one end of the yard. Several coal-blackened carts were parked in a row. Mandy tried to picture the ponies that once pulled the heavily laden carts through the underground passages.

Against one of the walls was a forge. Mandy closed her eyes and imagined a huge fire roaring in the furnace and a blacksmith pounding lumps of red-hot iron into horseshoes. For a moment, she even thought she could hear the ring of the hammer on iron. The loud metallic ringing persisted. Mandy realized suddenly that it was not in her imagination. She opened her eyes to see James banging two bits of rusty iron together.

"What are you doing that for?" She laughed.

"Sorry. But you looked like you were dreaming." He grinned. "And I thought you'd like to meet the black-smith." He gestured toward the forge.

A very old man had come in and was busy at the fur-nace. Mandy and James went over and saw that he was stoking up a fire. He greeted them as they approached.

"Hello," he said in a raspy voice. "Etherington's the name."

Mandy and James greeted him in turn. "Do you still shoe horses here?" asked Mandy, surprised to see that the forge was still in use.

"No," said Mr. Etherington. "I just show visitors how it was back when the mine was working. In those days, I used to work around the clock making shoes for the

ponies — the uneven, rocky ground in the tunnels was very hard on their hooves. Nowadays, I just make a few shoes a day and we sell them in the gift shop."

The blacksmith rolled up his sleeves as the coals caught fire and Mandy could see that, despite his age, the old man had bulging arm muscles. "It must have been very hard work," she said.

"Yes, it was tiring all right, but it was honest work," said Mr. Etherington, sliding a long leather apron over his head.

"What about the ponies?" asked Mandy anxiously. "What kind of lives did they have?"

Mr. Etherington poked the fire a little, then turned around. "To be honest," he said, "they had a really hard life. Most of them lived underground their whole lives and many worked very long shifts."

"Oh, how awful!" exclaimed Mandy, making a few notes on the clipboard she'd brought with her.

"Do you mean they never came up to the surface?" asked James, shocked. Like Mandy, he loved animals and was always interested in their welfare.

"Well, about once a year or so they were brought up for a vacation," Mr. Etherington explained. "But I sometimes wondered if that wasn't worse than leaving them underground."

"Why?" asked Mandy, biting the end of her pen.

"A lot of them were terrified by the bright light of day when they came up. And then, just when they'd gotten used to being in the open and were relaxing in the green fields, they had to go back down in the pit," the blacksmith told her.

"That's so cruel!" exclaimed Mandy.

"Perhaps life wasn't too bad for them underground," suggested James. "After all, the miners must have liked having ponies as coworkers. Were they well treated?" he asked the old man.

"That all depended on their handlers," Mr. Etherington replied. "Some of them really loved their ponies, but a few could be really cruel. You could see when a pony was well looked after. He'd do anything for his master."

"What happened to the ponies when the mine didn't need them anymore?" asked Mandy.

"Most of them went to live at sanctuaries run by horse protection societies," answered Mr. Etherington. "In fact, there's a refuge close by. It's called Sunfield Pony Sanctuary."

Mandy was amazed. She'd read that the pit ponies had been phased out many years ago. It hadn't occurred to her that any were still alive.

Mr. Etherington continued, "There are some happy pit ponies living out in the fresh air at Sunfield, but they're all in their golden years now." He shook a load of coal from a scuttle onto the fire, then pointed up a short flight of stairs. "If you want to find out more about our ponies, there's a whole display dedicated to them in the gallery," he said.

Mandy and James ran up the stairs and had just started reading about the first pony when a harsh buzzing sounded over the PA system.

"The bell! We'd better hurry," said James urgently. He shot down the stairs and hurtled toward the entrance.

"Wait for me!" cried Mandy.

As they ran past the forge, Mr. Etherington called to them. "Before you go, here's something for you." He held out two miniature horseshoes.

"They're beautiful," said Mandy, taking them from the blacksmith. "Thank you, Mr. Etherington."

"They're for good luck," he said solemnly. "You never know when you might need it."

"Well, I feel lucky already." Mandy smiled as she and James hurried toward the elevator shaft.

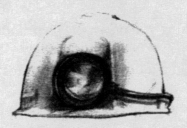

Two

The elevator was nothing like the ones Mandy was used to. It was a big box made out of thick planks that were bolted together on a strong-looking steel frame.

"It looks like a cage," Mandy said to James, as they waited with their classmates to enter the elevator.

"And that's just what we call it," said a burly man who was making his way through the excited group. He was wearing black overalls and tough work boots. On his head was a white safety helmet with a lamp attached to the front.

"Morning, all," he said, reaching the front of the group. "I'm Arthur Bradley. I used to work the coal

beds. I'll be taking you down the shaft today and showing you the ropes. Is everyone here?"

Ms. Potter did a quick head count. "Yes, all present,"
she told him.

"All right," said Arthur. "Before you get into the cage,
you'll need to get a lamp." He pointed to his helmet. "I'm
going to give you all one of these, then I'll show you
how to adjust the lamp."

Christie, who was in James's class, put up her hand.
"Is it *very* dark down there?" she asked nervously.

Arthur smiled. "Let's just say that it's not like a sunny
day at Scarborough. There *are* lights in the tunnels, but
they're not very bright. Anyway, it's a good idea to have
your own — just in case there's a power failure."

Mandy grimaced at James. "I don't think I'd like that,"
she murmured.

One by one, they all filed past Arthur, who handed
them their helmets before they entered the cage. Everyone was in high spirits, chatting eagerly about what
they could expect to see when they reached the bottom
of the shaft. Mandy put on her helmet and switched on
the lamp. She ran her hands over the planks next to her.
They were smooth and blackened from years of use.
The steel floor was dusty and rang out like a drum as
the dozens of feet clattered over it.

At last everyone got their helmet and Arthur climbed

into the cage, pulling the gate shut behind him. The noisy chatter stopped abruptly. There was a trembling motion as Arthur operated the controls, then suddenly they felt themselves plunging rapidly into the pitch-black darkness. Mandy's stomach seemed to lurch up into her mouth. The feeling reminded her of some of the really awesome rides in amusement parks — only this was the real thing, not just a game.

Then, quite unexpectedly because no one could see around them, there was a loud thud and a sudden jolt as the cage hit the firmness of the floor at the end of the drop.

"Phew," said James, as Arthur unlocked the gate and the group began to filter out of the elevator. "That was quite a drop!"

Mandy laughed at James's amazed face. "I wonder how far down we are?" she asked.

"Almost one and a quarter miles," said Arthur, over-hearing her question.

"Wow! That's almost as far as Welford is from Walton," said James, as he and Mandy took their first steps along the tunnel.

In contrast to the cool air on the way down, it was very warm at the bottom of the shaft. Mandy unzipped her jacket, wishing she'd left it in the coatroom above ground. She breathed in deeply. The air was thick and carried a stale smell of coal. She peered down the tunnel ahead of her. Lamps were attached to the walls every few feet, giving off a dim yellow light. As her eyes became used to the shadowy gloom, she could see that the tunnel was about seven feet high and six feet wide. On the ground, a narrow set of rails ran off into the darkness beyond.

"We're in the largest passageway — it's known as the main heading," Arthur announced and his voice sounded flat in the close and stuffy atmosphere. "This tunnel leads to the main coal beds but there are also a few narrow side passages leading off it. Some are emergency escape routes and others are tunnels that were worked by the miners. We'll keep to the main heading, though — the smaller tunnels aren't lit up."

Arthur started off down the main heading, the light from his headlamp bouncing against the rough side walls of the tunnel. "Keep together, everyone," he said. "Please don't wander away from the group."

"I don't think anyone will want to do that," said James.

"No." Mandy chuckled. "It would be a little too spooky on your own." She stepped carefully on the uneven floor. An invisible pothole made her stumble and, as she got her balance, she thought about what Mr.

Etherington had said about the ground being rough on the ponies' feet.

"On the floor, you can see a pair of rails," Arthur pointed out. "Before the mine was mechanized, ponies used to drag tubs of coal from the seam, where it was mined, along the rails to the bottom of a shaft. There, the coal was tipped into a cage to be hoisted to the surface. The pony would then drag the empty tub back to the seam where his handler would fasten another full tub to the harness, before driving the pony back to the cage."

"How long did the ponies have to work?" asked Mandy.

"Well, a shift was usually eight hours but sometimes ponies worked double shifts," Arthur explained.

"That's terrible," cried Mandy. She was furious at the thought of the ponies being taken advantage of. "There should have been a law against it!"

"There *was* a law," Arthur said. "Double shifts were illegal, but a few mine bosses just disregarded the laws when it came to ponies. You see, the ponies were cheap labor. One did the work of three men. But instead of being grateful and making sure the ponies were well rested after a hard shift, a few bosses sometimes tried to get even more work out of the poor things."

"It's a shame they couldn't go on strike — like the miners did sometimes," said James.

There were a few bursts of laughter at James's suggestion.

"Actually," Arthur said, "in a way, some of the ponies tried to do just that. They could be really stubborn at times, even refusing to budge. But mostly, they were very willing workers."

Hearing this, Mandy felt even more indignant. After all, if the ponies were so willing, their handlers should have treasured them, not taken advantage of them.

The group came to a fork in the tunnel and Arthur led them to the right. After a short distance, the ground suddenly seemed to fall away beneath them and they soon found themselves going down a steep slope. The roof was lower than before and the walls were so close that everyone had to walk in single file. The wall lamps were much farther apart, making the passage dimmer. Mandy could only just see Arthur a few feet ahead of her in the gloom.

"This is the oldest part of the main heading," Arthur said, as the group stumbled along.

"That's for sure," joked James. "The air in here must be as old as the tunnel."

"Uh-huh," agreed Mandy. "It's really stuffy." She looked over her shoulder. The flickering headlamps behind her cast an eerie glow. She could hardly recognize some of her friends. In the dim and shadowy half-light, their faces looked really strange. *Almost like gargoyles!* Mandy thought. On the walls, their shadows loomed large, vanished, then reappeared as the lamp beams bobbed up and down. Suddenly, someone bumped into one of the wall lamps and it smashed to the ground. There was a dull thud, and then a few screams.

"What is it?" called Mandy, straining her eyes to try to see what was going on.

"It's Christie," called one of Mandy's classmates, Susan Collins. "I think she's fainted. Where's Ms. Potter?"

There was much commotion as Ms. Potter wove her way from the rear of the group to where Christie lay unconscious on the rough ground. Arthur came back to see what had happened.

"What happened?" asked Ms. Potter anxiously, kneeling down beside the girl.

"I don't know," said Susan. "She got a little nervous when we started going down the hill. And then she just collapsed."

"It's most likely just a touch of claustrophobia," suggested Arthur reassuringly. "It happens down here pretty often."

"Christie," said Ms. Potter soothingly. "Christie. Can you hear me?"

Everyone clustered around Ms. Potter and Christie, pushing one another as they all tried to get a glimpse of their unconscious friend.

"Could you all move back a little and give me some room?" said Ms. Potter, sounding rather agitated. "Otherwise, I'll get claustrophobic, too."

Mandy and James took a few steps back into the darkness.

"Let's go in a little deeper," James whispered to Mandy. "Nobody's paying any attention to us."

"Okay," said Mandy. "But let's not go too far, in case we get lost."

The two friends moved off quietly down the murky passage. The hubbub behind them gradually receded until it was just a faint hum.

"We shouldn't get out of earshot. Come on, let's go back," said Mandy after a while, her voice echoing in the narrow space around them.

"Wait," said James. "Look here." He shone his headlamp against the wall. The small beam of light flashed across the glistening black rock face, then suddenly faded into nothingness.

As Mandy stared at the vanishing ray of light, she became aware of a shape in the wall. "It looks like a hole in the rock," she said.

"I think it's one of those side tunnels that Arthur was telling us about," said James. "Let's investigate. Maybe I'll find out something useful for my project."

Mandy looked back up the main tunnel. The headlamps belonging to the rest of the group shone like small beacons. Mandy could still make out Ms. Potter's voice asking Christie if she felt better.

"All right," said Mandy. "But we'd better hurry. It sounds like Christie's coming around."

"Let's just have a quick look to see what it's like," said James.

The two friends stepped cautiously through the hole, which was surrounded by a rough timber framework. They found themselves in a very narrow, unlit tunnel. The sides brushed against Mandy's arms as she inched her way along.

"Imagine spending your life working in a place like this!" said James. Before Mandy could comment, his words echoed back at them both, ". . . *like this! . . . like this! . . . like this!*"

"Wow!" said James, sounding a little unnerved. "*Wow! Wow! Wow!*"

Mandy giggled quietly and moved forward into the pitch-blackness, her muffled chuckles bouncing back at her until they faded away, leaving a heavy silence in the air. As the silence deepened, Mandy suddenly became aware of a presence. Something strong and powerful was surrounding her and filled the dark void ahead. Was someone else in the tunnel with them?

She stared into the darkness beyond, but could see nothing. She looked over her shoulder and the beam from her headlamp lit up only James's face. Mandy shone the lamp all around her, but it illuminated only the emptiness in the tunnel. Yet, somehow, she couldn't shake off the feeling that they were not alone. A shiver trickled down her spine.

"There's someone here with us," she whispered to James. "*With us, with us, with us*," hissed Mandy's words.

"I can't see anyone," whispered James cautiously.

"Shh, let's listen," replied Mandy.

They stood dead still. Mandy concentrated hard, listening for the sound of a footfall or the rustle of clothing against the walls. But not even the faintest sound disturbed the stillness.

"There's nothing here," said James after a few seconds. "It must be your imagination."

Mandy shook her head. "I'm not sure," she said. "There's something eerie about this place." She listened again. Then, shrugging her shoulders, she said, "I guess you're right. After all, it is pretty creepy in here."

"Well, we've seen what a side tunnel is like now," said James. "We'd better get back to the others."

Mandy eased herself around and, just as she began to follow James toward the main heading, she became aware of a faint sound. Slowly, she realized that it was the sound of distant hooves. She stopped and looked back down the dark tunnel. The clopping sound came closer. She held her breath and listened keenly again. The noise was definitely heading their way! Then, suddenly, it stopped, leaving a silence so heavy that Mandy could hear the regular thudding of her own heartbeat and the rhythmic sound of James's breathing as he moved quietly toward the tunnel entrance.

But what had made that strange sound and why had it stopped so suddenly?

The warm, clammy air had folded itself around Mandy like a blanket. She tried to take a deep breath but the air seemed to stick in her throat. Her headlamp flickered and went out. For a second, a wave of panic washed over her. Then, without warning, her headlamp came back on, revealing a sight that made her heart miss a beat. Staring at her out of the eerie blackness was a pair of eyes. They pierced the darkness like lasers and shone right into Mandy's own eyes. She couldn't move. The bright stare had transfixed her and seemed to penetrate deep into her very soul.

Mandy gasped and, just as suddenly as the eyes had appeared, they vanished, leaving the darkness unbroken once more. She blinked. Movement returned to her legs. She took a few paces backward, then turned and scrambled toward the hole in the wall. James had already climbed through and was waiting for her in the main tunnel.

"Did you see?" she gasped, as she hurried through the hole.

"What?" asked James, looking puzzled.

"Those eyes — shining in the darkness. You must have seen them," Mandy insisted.

James scratched his head, then pushed back his hair. "I didn't see anything," he said.

"Well, that's probably because you were heading back up the tunnel," said Mandy. "You *must* have heard the hooves, though. Didn't you?"

"Hooves? What are you talking about, Mandy?" asked her friend, his forehead creased in confusion. "Come on. We'd better get back." James shook his head and set off toward the rest of the group.

"I'm talking about the clip-clopping sound I heard back there," Mandy replied, running to keep up with him.

"Eyes shining out of the darkness and horses' hooves! Are you sure you're okay?" asked James, stopping for a second to let Mandy catch up with him.

"I'm fine!" stressed Mandy. She took hold of James's sleeve. "Look, I know what I saw and heard. They were real. There was something in that tunnel with us."

"Maybe you did see something," said James quietly. "But you said yourself that it was creepy back there. Maybe you were claustrophobic — like Christie — and that made you see and hear things that weren't there."

Mandy thought for a moment. James's suggestion

made sense. Maybe he was right. After all, *he* hadn't heard or seen anything unusual. And it *was* very stuffy in the side tunnel. Perhaps there hadn't been enough oxygen in there and her mind had played tricks on her. *I think I'll read up on claustrophobia when I get home*, she thought.

They reached the others just as Ms. Potter was helping Christie to her feet. No one had noticed Mandy and James's absence, because they had all been too concerned about Christie. She leaned on Ms. Potter's arm as they made their way toward the elevator shaft. Mandy lengthened her stride until she'd caught up with Christie.

"Are you feeling better?" she asked her.

Christie turned and looked at Mandy. Even in the dim light, Mandy could see that she was very pale.

"I guess so," said Christie quietly.

Seeing Christie looking so pale and shaken, Mandy knew instantly that her own experience in the tunnel had not been the same as Christie's. Unlike her classmate, she was not trembling and weak. She did feel a little disturbed, but there was also something thrilling about her strange encounter in the tunnel. She looked back over her shoulder. The dull yellow light looked different somehow. It seemed to have taken on a mysterious shimmer and, deeper along the tunnel where there should have been absolute blackness, there was a soft white glow. But who would believe her? Even James was skeptical.

The group reached the elevator shaft and Mandy looked back one more time. She knew in her heart that they weren't leaving behind an empty maze. Somewhere in the depths of the mine was a mysterious presence. And she was convinced that what she'd seen and heard was a pony.

Three

An icy draft forced its way down the shaft as the elevator climbed slowly to the surface.

"It's even colder and windier in here than when we went down," Mandy said to James.

"Maybe that's because we got used to the heat in the tunnel," James suggested.

The elevator lurched to a stop and Arthur pulled open the gate with a clatter. The group emerged, blinking, into the daylight to find that a swirling wind had pushed away the sunny brightness of the morning.

Mandy shivered and zipped up her jacket. "It looks very stormy," she shivered.

Overhead, towering black clouds gathered threateningly. It was quite a surprise to find conditions so different from earlier. It reminded Mandy of how strange she felt when she went to the movies in daylight and came out afterward into the darkness of evening.

The two friends leaned into the biting wind and hurried to the shelter of the exhibition hall, where they wandered around looking at the various exhibits. James was fascinated by a display of computers that had controlled the coal-cleaning process, but Mandy found it hard to concentrate on the various items on display. She couldn't forget her strange experience in the tunnel.

They came to a set of photographs that showed the history of the mine.

"Look at those funny old trucks," said James. He pointed to a faded picture of several old-fashioned bulky vehicles piled high with coal and laughed.

"They're almost as funny as the clothes everyone is wearing." Mandy chuckled. Then she pointed to another picture. It showed an injured pony receiving veterinary treatment. The caption beneath the photograph explained how some ponies were injured underground — often because of rockfalls or because the tunnels were so narrow that the ponies' flanks were badly scraped. Mandy could see huge gashes on the injured pony's side. They looked very painful.

"Do you think the ponies were allowed to rest while their wounds were healing?" Mandy wondered.

"Maybe we can ask the blacksmith," said James.

But there wasn't any time to return to the yard. The second group had returned from the depths of the mine and the teachers were eager to get going before the storm came.

Heavy drops of rain began to fall as the bus set off. There were ominous rumblings from the dark sky and before long they were driving through a torrential downpour. The storm seemed to have put everyone in a solemn mood and hardly anyone spoke during the ride home.

Mandy found herself deep in thought. Now that she'd seen for herself how harsh the conditions were underground, she couldn't get the pit ponies out of her mind. Nor could she forget what she was sure that she'd seen in the side tunnel.

James nudged her with his elbow. "Still thinking about those shining eyes?" He grinned.

Mandy sighed, then smiled. "Yes, but you must have been right. Maybe I *was* imagining things. After all, *you* didn't see or hear anything unusual."

James took off his glasses and cleaned a few specks of coal dust off them. "Maybe what you saw was just the reflection of your headlamp against the rocks or on a metal hook or something in the wall."

"And the sound of hooves?" asked Mandy.

"I don't know. Echoes of everyone's footsteps? Remember the echoes in that small tunnel? *Tunnel, tunnel, tunnel,*" said James playfully.

Mandy laughed. It was just like James to come up with a practical solution! "Okay. You win. There must be a sensible explanation to it all," she agreed. Then, changing the subject, she added, "Are you definitely going to choose tunneling for your project?"

"I think so," James told her. "I'm going to find out how tunnels are made and also about the different kinds of tunnels."

"I didn't see much useful information at the museum," Mandy said thoughtfully.

"Me, neither," said James. "I wish we'd had more time. I'm sure there's tons of useful stuff on the Internet, though. Dad said he might be able to fix the computer problem today. With any luck, I'll be able to search the World Wide Web tonight!"

"I wish we could get connected at Animal Ark," said Mandy a little enviously. "But Dad says the only web we have time for is on a duck's foot!"

"I tell you what, if Dad does fix the problem, why

don't you come over after school tomorrow and we'll do a search together," suggested James. "That way, you can decide exactly what you want to download."

"That would be great," said Mandy.

Later, Mandy told her parents all about the trip. It was dinnertime and they were sitting around the big pine table in the kitchen.

"It must be really eerie in the tunnels," Dr. Emily said. "The ponies that worked down there would have to be very calm."

"Yes, not a place for a nervous pony," agreed Dr. Adam, pouring himself another glass of iced tea. "But, even for easygoing horses, I can't imagine that a life in a coal mine would have been much fun."

"Some of them got badly injured scraping their sides on the walls of the narrow tunnels," said Mandy, remembering the photograph they'd seen of the pony being looked after by a vet. "But at least there aren't any ponies working underground anymore."

"Would you believe that some of them are still alive?" said Dr. Emily, as she began to clear the table.

"That's what the blacksmith told me," Mandy said, smiling. "And he said there's a refuge near the mine called Sunfield Pony Sanctuary. I'd love to go there and meet the ponies."

Dr. Adam got up and started to wash the dishes. "That would be really interesting," he said. "Perhaps we can visit Sunfield. I'll try to find out about opening times."

"Thanks, Dad. You're the best!" said Mandy, giving him a warm hug. She dried the dishes, then noticed a bowl of leftovers on the table. "I'll just give this to the birds," she said and went outside to sprinkle the food on the lawn.

The storm raged wildly. Mandy battled through the roaring gale, barely able to stand up straight. It was so dark and misty, she could hardly see her hands in front of her. She wished that she wasn't alone. She pictured the cozy, warm kitchen at home with the fire glowing comfortingly in the fireplace. She knew that her mom would be anxious about her being out in this weather and that there would be a big mug of hot chocolate waiting for her when she returned.

She leaned into the wind and tried to hurry, but the cruel and icy blast just pushed her back. She was making no headway at all. Beads of sweat broke out on her forehead and a tingle of fear ran through her. She turned and tried to retrace her footsteps, but the gale pushed her back from that direction, too.

She tried to go forward again but the wall of wind was solid. She could not break through it. All around

her, the storm boiled and seethed, enclosing her in its whirling anger. She knew she was trapped.

Suddenly, amid the howling of the wind and the vicious crack of the thunderclaps, came a new sound. It started faintly. Mandy closed her eyes and tried to block out the roar of the storm and concentrate on this new sound. Perhaps it was someone coming to rescue her. Gradually, the sound grew clearer, taking shape above the noise all around. It was the sound of a pony whinnying. Urgent, persistent whinnying that bore into Mandy's hearing, like a machine drilling into her head.

She opened her eyes at once. She was sweating and gasping for breath. The storm had vanished but the sound still rang loudly in her ears. She looked around. She was in her own bed and the noise was coming from the alarm clock on her bedside table. She leaned over and switched off the alarm, then sighed and rested her head in her hands. What a frightening dream! And so real! The animal had sounded so distressed.

She pushed off her comforter, then went over to the window and drew back the curtains. The sun was just beginning to climb above the eastern horizon, lighting up a sky that was blue and clear. There was no sign of yesterday's storm. It must have passed during the night. Even though Mandy's dad had picked her up after the trip, she'd gotten thoroughly drenched just running from the bus to the Animal Ark Land Rover. No wonder she'd had that nightmare!

She showered, then pulled on her school uniform. As she sat brushing her short blond hair, her eyes came to rest on the miniature horseshoe Mr. Etherington had

given her at the mine the day before. She'd hung it over
the mirror until she could decide on a more permanent
place for it.

She reached for the horseshoe. The little iron arc fit-
ted snugly in the palm of her hand. As far as she could
tell, it was an exact replica of the real thing. She ran a
finger over the smooth surface and around the edges of
the holes that, in a real shoe, were for the nails that
would attach the shoe to the horse's hoof.

As her finger traced the outline of the horseshoe,
Mandy became aware of a raised pattern around the
curve of the arc. She looked closely and saw that there
was a word carved into the metal. The letters were so
small that she couldn't make out what the word was.
She pulled a magnifying glass out of a drawer and
looked through it: DEFENDER.

Defender? What could that mean? Maybe it was a
business name that the museum used.

As she sat looking at the tiny shoe, her thoughts ran
to the pit ponies. Then she remembered that she was
going home with James after school to search the Internet for more information about them. He had called last
night to say that his dad had figured out what the problem was. She checked the time. It was getting late. She
replaced the horseshoe, then grabbed her schoolbag
and ran downstairs for breakfast.

*   *   *

"Guess what our password is?" James was beaming with delight, as he got ready to connect to the Internet later that afternoon.

"Football?" suggested Mandy, who had pulled a chair up alongside James at the desk.

"No," James said, laughing. "Guess again."

The door to the study was pushed open and James's black Labrador, Blackie, came in, with his tail wagging frantically and a feather in his mouth.

"And here's a clue," said James, swiveling around in his chair.

"Blackie?" Mandy chuckled. "I should have guessed the first time!"

James typed BLACKIE into the space for the password. A series of strange beeping sounds came from the modem as it dialed the number to connect the computer to the Internet. Blackie frowned and spat out the feather, then tilted his head first to one side then to the other, trying to make out the strange new noise. He growled softly, then, jumping up and putting his front paws on James's lap, started to bark at the modem.

James laughed and pushed him down. "You'd better get used to it, boy," James said. "You're going to be hearing it a lot. Okay, Mandy, we're on-line now. Let's do a search for pit ponies."

There were dozens of pages giving information on pit ponies and other animals that were used in the mines. Mandy and James learned that canaries in cages were used to warn miners of poisonous gas, like methane, underground. If the canaries died in the tunnels, it usually meant that there was a buildup of methane that could cause an explosion. This was a clear signal to the miners to head for the surface right away.

"Oh, how awful for the canaries," said Mandy. "They never stood a chance of escaping. It's so sad that they had to be sacrificed like that."

"I suppose they rely on modern technology in mines to warn the miners of danger now," said James, scrolling down a page. "Hey, look at this. It says here that at the beginning of the twentieth century there were nearly a hundred thousand ponies working underground."

"What!" exclaimed Mandy, then she read farther down the page. "And here it says that their average life span was only seven years. *Seven years!* That's so young. I read that Shetlands can live to be more than thirty years old. That just proves how hard pit ponies' lives must have been underground."

"At least we know that a lot of them went on to live normal lives in sanctuaries," said James.

The two friends scanned a few more sites and printed

out some details Mandy thought would be useful, then James searched for information on tunneling. After a while, he disconnected from the Internet. "I'd better not spend too much time on it," he said. "Dad made me promise not to ring up a huge phone bill."

The door opened and Mrs. Hunter came into the study. "Your dad's on the phone, Mandy. He says he's been trying to get through for the last twenty minutes, but the phone's been busy the whole time!" She smiled at James. "I'll have to make sure I make all my calls while you're at school!"

"Sorry, Mom," said James sheepishly.

"That's all right," said his mother. "I think this Internet thing is fabulous — just as long as you use it for your schoolwork. Anyway, Mandy, your dad says he's got a surprise for you."

Mandy followed Mrs. Hunter into the hallway. "Hi," she said, picking up the receiver. She listened for a minute, then cried, "Thanks! I'll tell James right now."

She hung up and ran back to the study. "Dad's been in touch with the Sunfield Pony Sanctuary," she told James. "They said we can visit anytime we like, so Dad's arranged for us to go there this Saturday. Do you want to come, too?"

"You bet!" said James eagerly.

Mandy gathered together the printouts of the pages

James had downloaded for her. From one of the pages, a bay Shetland pony wearing a heavy harness and dragging a full load of coal stared out mournfully at Mandy. Three miners stood next to the pony, petting him on his neck. "Poor thing," she sighed. "I hope your life wasn't too bad. And at least there are *some* pit ponies leading happy lives now. I can hardly wait to meet them on Saturday!"

Four

Sunfield Pony Sanctuary stood amid green, rolling hills a few miles beyond Amberton.

"I'll open it," said Mandy, as Dr. Adam pulled up in front of the big wooden gate at the entrance to the sanctuary.

She hopped out and swung open the heavy gate. Then, once her dad had driven through, she checked that the latch was firmly down before climbing back into the Land Rover. They drove over a cattle crossing and followed a winding driveway to the office. All around them were lush paddocks where ponies, horses, and even a few donkeys grazed contentedly.

"They're not all pit ponies, are they?" asked James.

"I don't think so," Dr. Adam replied. He stopped the Land Rover in a parking area next to the office. "A sanctuary like this might rescue horses from all sorts of situations."

"Some of them might even be abandoned racehorses or polo ponies, I suppose," suggested Mandy.

"Probably," her father said.

They crunched across the gravel toward the office. Mandy breathed in deeply, savoring the rich, earthy scent of horses.

Dr. Adam pushed open the office door. Inside, a short, weathered-looking man was speaking on the telephone. He seemed to be in a state of panic and didn't even notice the visitors. A girl about Mandy's age, wearing overalls and riding boots, was standing next to the man. She had her back to the door and didn't see Mandy, James, and Dr. Adam come in, either.

"Well, do you know when he *will* be back?" the man was saying to someone at the other end of the telephone. "*This evening!* That'll be too late. You're sure that you can't get ahold of him?" The man listened for a minute, then put the phone down. "I don't believe it!" he exclaimed gruffly to the young girl. "The vet's away at an equine conference in Bradford and his partner has been called to an emergency on a stud farm fifty miles away." He opened a book and began flipping anxiously through the pages.

Mandy recognized the book as from the shelves at Animal Ark. It was called *A Veterinary Guide to Horse Care.*

"You're sure it looks like colic, Ceri?" said the man.

The girl nodded. "He's not eating, but he must be in a lot of pain because he keeps kicking at his belly with his hind legs. He'd just started to roll on the ground when I left him to come and tell you."

"Sounds like colic, all right! We can't waste any time," said the man. He looked up from the book and for the first time noticed Mandy, James, and Dr. Adam. "Sorry, folks, we've got a bit of an emergency here. You're going to have to come back later."

"I don't want to intrude," began Dr. Adam politely, "but I think I can help you."

The man looked at him sharply. "Do you know of another vet?" he asked eagerly.

"Actually, I *am* a vet," answered Dr. Adam. "And from what Ceri says, I'm sure your horse does have colic. You're right, there's no time to waste. The horse needs emergency treatment or I'm afraid you could lose him." He turned to Mandy. "Get my bag, will you, Mandy?"

Mandy dashed out of the office. It was a good thing her dad took his bag with him everywhere. She heaved it out of the back of the Land Rover. The bag contained instruments and medication that could be used in most types of emergencies. She returned to the office just as the others were coming out of the door.

"He's in the paddock down by the river," Ceri told Dr. Adam, and they all set off in that direction. "His racing name is Woodward's Challenge, but we call him Woody."

Even from a few hundred feet away, Mandy could make out which horse was in trouble. Near the far side of the paddock, a big chestnut stallion had thrown himself to the ground and was rolling and struggling in pain. "Oh, how terrible!" she exclaimed. "Hurry, Dad."

"It does look as if Woody's in bad shape," agreed Dr. Adam as they climbed through the railing. "I just hope there are no complications. Colic is much simpler to deal with if the pain is mostly due to air in his stomach."

Mandy crossed her fingers. She knew that complicated cases of colic needed immediate surgery and that, even then, some horses didn't survive.

"Don't worry, Mandy," said James reassuringly as they rushed across the stubby, freshly cut grass. "You know that your dad's a great vet. He'll make Woody feel better, if anyone can."

The horse was back on his feet and standing quietly by the time they reached him.

"He's between bouts of pain right now," said Dr. Adam, opening his bag and taking out a stethoscope and thermometer. "That gives me some time to examine him. Will someone hold the bridle, please?"

Mandy and James each took hold of a cheek piece, on either side of the horse's head, while Ceri soothingly stroked his neck.

Dr. Adam listened to the stallion's heart and checked his temperature. "Hmm, his heart rate and temperature are a little high," he said. He looked at the horse's eyes and inside his mouth, muttering, "A little on the pale side," then carefully examined his belly and flanks. "Pretty swollen," he murmured. "It's definitely a case of acute indigestion. I'll give him some injections to relieve the pain, then look at him more closely."

He prepared three syringes and one by one injected them into the horse, all the while speaking softly to him. "There now, boy," he said, gently rubbing the skin where he'd pushed in the needles. "That should help you." He put the syringes into a special disposal bag, then looked around. "Let's give him some space while the painkillers work."

Mandy and James pulled themselves up on the railing and sat watching the powerful chestnut horse. "He's a beauty," said Mandy to Ceri, who was leaning against the railing next to her.

"Yes, he's an ex-racehorse, but he was being badly treated so we rescued him. He came in only yesterday," Ceri told her.

"Ah, that might explain the colic," said Dr. Adam. "Woody could have been a little stressed when he arrived — even hungry — and might have eaten his food too quickly and then been too tired to digest it properly. It's a good thing you picked up on the signs, Ceri. It might have been a lot worse if you hadn't."

Dr. Adam went back to the horse and began to examine him thoroughly. After a few minutes, he called to Mandy. "Get me a long stomach tube from the bag, please, Mandy."

Mandy pulled out a plastic tube and handed it to her dad, then watched as he gently inserted it into the horse's nose and gradually fed it down into his stomach. After a while, the horse seemed to relax and Dr. Adam listened once more to his heart rate. "That's better," he said. "Almost back to normal." He unhooked the stethoscope and turned to the man. "He's out of immediate danger and there don't seem to be any problems. It's a classic case of colic. But he'll need to be on medication and a special diet for a few days. Make sure he's rested and kept warm."

The man shook Dr. Adam's hand warmly. "Thanks so

much. I don't know what we'd have done if you hadn't shown up when you did."

Dr. Adam smiled. "I'm glad to have been able to help."

"Um, would you mind sending the bill in the mail?" the man asked, sounding embarrassed. "You see, we're a little low on funds at the moment. I'm hoping for a few donations to come in within the next couple of weeks."

"I wouldn't dream of charging you," said Dr. Adam.

The man looked relieved. "That's very kind of you."

"And I think you're very kind to rescue pit ponies," added Mandy cheerfully.

"Well, it's very nice of you to say so," said the man and then he snapped his fingers. "Now I know who you are. You're the people who called me from Welford the other day, aren't you? And you want to see some pit ponies!" He scratched his balding head and then said, "Hope? Wasn't that the name?"

Dr. Adam smiled and nodded. "Adam Hope. And this is my daughter, Mandy, and her friend James Hunter. Mandy needs to find out about the ponies for her school project."

"And I'm Paul Newbury. Ceri is my granddaughter." He smiled fondly at her. "She's my right-hand girl. Comes almost every weekend to help me out. I'd be lost without her."

Ceri grinned shyly. "That's not true. You know more about horses than I ever will." She looked at Mandy and James. "Grandad used to be one of the country's top jockeys, you know."

"Of course!" said Dr. Adam. "I thought I recognized that name. But didn't you retire early?"

"Yes," said Mr. Newbury. "I saw what was happening to many horses in the name of recreation and industry. All the racehorses abandoned when they stopped winning big money for their owners; polo ponies whipped brutally by some harsh trainers; old mares left without food when they could no longer breed — I could go on and on." He shook his head sadly, then took a deep breath. "I didn't want to be part of it. So I pulled out and looked for a way to help unwanted and mistreated horses. That's how I ended up here at Sunfield."

"A worthy change of career," Dr. Adam said sincerely. He turned back to the horse, who was standing calmly, swishing his tail slowly from side to side. Dr. Adam patted him firmly on the shoulder and said, "Let's get you into a stall so that you can rest quietly and get over the shock."

Mandy and James helped Ceri to lead the stallion to the stable block nearest the office. Dr. Adam and Paul Newbury walked behind them, discussing the treatment the horse would need over the next few days. "If he shows any signs of an infection, you'll need to contact a vet immediately," said Dr. Adam.

Soon the horse was comfortably settled and Mr. Newbury suggested that they go back to the office for a cup of coffee. "And some of Ceri's homemade cookies," he added. "There's nothing to beat them this side of town."

"That sounds good," said Dr. Adam, rubbing his hands together. "Are you joining us?" he asked Mandy and James. "Or are you too excited to see the ponies?"

Mandy laughed. "What do you think, Dad?"

James also wanted to see the ponies first, so Ceri offered to take them both around the sanctuary.

"Will you take us to meet the pit ponies first?" Mandy asked Ceri.

As they made their way toward a paddock on the far side of the sanctuary, Ceri told them what she knew about the pit ponies. "Most of them have been here for years and years," she said. "I think the last ones came to Sunfield about twenty-five years ago. But they're still as fit as fiddles, thanks to my grandad. He spends money on his ponies before he spends anything on himself!"

There were about a dozen ponies in the large paddock. Most of them were sturdy little Shetlands, but there were also a few beautiful Welsh mountain ponies. Seeing them arrive, two Shetlands — one brown and the other black — came trotting purposefully over to the railing. They pushed their heads over the bottom railing and began nuzzling at Mandy's and James's outstretched hands.

"I know what you want," Mandy said, laughing. She reached into her coat pocket for some sugar lumps she'd brought with her and held them out to the ponies on her flattened palm.

While the ponies crunched up the sugar lumps, Ceri told Mandy and James about the pair. "This is Margot," she said, patting the brown pony's neck, "and this is Duke." She ran her fingers through his thick, shaggy mane, which flopped forward on the black pony's forehead. "Grandad says they've been inseparable since the day they came here from Amberton."

Almost as if he'd understood what Ceri had said, Duke nibbled Margot's neck affectionately.

"They must be very old," observed Mandy. She had noticed that Duke's teeth were very long.

"Yes, they're both about thirty-eight. They came here when they were about eleven or twelve," Ceri told her. "They're a little like an old married couple," she laughed. "Grandad even calls them Mr. and Mrs.!"

Margot snorted a few times, then began nudging James's jacket pocket, looking for more treats.

"All right, all right!" exclaimed James. "Give me a

chance." He pulled out two apples, which the ponies gobbled up at once.

"I'll take you to meet some others," said Ceri, climbing through the railing.

Mandy and James followed her and, with Duke and Margot trotting closely by their sides, went with Ceri to the center of the paddock where three other ponies were eating hay from a trough.

As they reached the ponies, a chilly breeze suddenly sprang up, finding its way down Mandy's neck. She pulled up her collar, but the iciness clung to the back of her neck as if it had been trapped inside her coat. She looked up at the sky. A big, gray cloud had appeared from nowhere and was hovering menacingly overhead, blocking out the weak sunshine and casting a deep, gloomy shadow over the paddock. *I wonder if we're in for another storm*, thought Mandy.

"Have you got any more sugar lumps?" asked James, breaking into her thoughts. "I ran out."

All five of the ponies had encircled him and were vying for treats.

"You look like the Pied Piper," said Mandy with a laugh. She passed a handful of sugar lumps to James and was about to ask Ceri about the three other ponies when she felt a gentle nudge on the small of her back. She spun around and almost fell over a handsome strawberry-roan Shetland. "Hello," she said in surprise. "You crept up on me very quietly!"

The pony looked up at Mandy and gave her an intense stare. She'd brought an apple and offered it to the little horse. But he showed no interest in it at all and continued to stare at her. Mandy found she couldn't escape his gaze. She was compelled to return it. It was almost as if he'd mesmerized her.

Then something stirred deep within her memory. She struggled in her mind to grasp what it was. And all at once, it came to her. The pony was very familiar. Mandy had met him before. But where — and when?

Spellbound, she leaned forward to caress his neck and tried to figure out where she could have seen him.

At that moment, a strong ray of sunshine broke through the dark cloud above. Like a spotlight, it shone directly onto the pony, making him glow radiantly.

"Wow," exclaimed Mandy. "Your coat really shines in the sun!"

Overhearing Mandy's comment, Ceri turned around. "Oh, I see Flame has introduced himself to you," she laughed. It was as if her words had switched off the sunbeam, for it disappeared in an instant.

"You can say that again!" said Mandy, still puzzled by the pony's intense interest in her. "He's very forward!"

Ceri's interruption had also broken the mysterious,

invisible cord that had linked Mandy and Flame. The pony bucked his head and whinnied softly, then walked over to the trough to feed.

"Flame's one of Grandad's favorites," said Ceri. "He's been here since he was five, but he wasn't always this bold. Grandad says that when he first came out of the mine, he was really traumatized."

"Maybe he wasn't used to the daylight and wide-open spaces," said James. The ponies were still snuffling around his pockets, even though he'd turned them inside out to show that he had no more treats.

"Yes, he was frightened of everything — the light, the trees, the wind, other people — he wouldn't even eat at first and bolted whenever anyone came near him. But Grandad soon made him comfortable. He's got a magic touch with horses."

"Flame looks like a very sensitive pony," commented Mandy, unable to take her eyes off the horse.

"I think he is," said Ceri. "And he's very smart. Much smarter than most of the other horses here."

"Why do you say that?" asked James, pushing his pockets back into his pants. The ponies had given up trying to find more food on him and were standing quietly at his side.

"I don't know — it's just that he seems to know things that we don't know," Ceri answered. "Like when a storm's coming. Even if it's a bright, sunny day, he'll start getting all edgy and then we know that the weather's going to change. Grandad calls Flame his storm warning."

"A little like the weather forecasters on TV!" quipped James.

"Except that they always seem to be wrong." Mandy laughed.

Dr. Adam was waving to them from the office so they started walking back across the paddock. Before she ducked through the railing, Mandy turned and looked back at the ponies. Flame was standing alone, watching her. And once more he was bathed in light. Another ray of sun had broken through the cloud and was pouring itself down on the little pony.

Mandy felt strangely unsettled. Something mysterious had taken place in that paddock but she couldn't put her finger on it. It was as if she knew him, but how could they possibly have met before? And it was as if he knew her, too. There was definitely a bond between them. But why?

Five

Mandy knew, even in her sleep, that she was in the grip of another nightmare. But there was nothing she could do to get out of it. She couldn't even will herself to wake up.

Frightening images and sounds entered her mind, flinging her onto a roller coaster of terror. *"Somebody wake me up!"* she screamed as the fear closed in on her. Then, with a cry for help fading on her lips, she suddenly found herself awake.

Mandy sat up in bed. It was still dark, and dead quiet. A creaking sound from somewhere in the house startled her. She held her breath, then realized with relief that it was just one of the usual creaky noises in the old house.

She switched on her bedside lamp and looked at the time. It was three o'clock — hours to go before dawn. But the dream had left her wide awake. She didn't think she'd be able to go back to sleep again.

Mandy leaned back and closed her eyes. The frightening images that had disturbed her sleep were still fresh in her memory. She ran through the dream again

in her mind. She could still see and hear the chestnut Shetland pony that was in the dream so clearly. At first, the pony had been anxious as he walked through an underground tunnel. Then he became more and more distressed, rearing and bucking with fear. He tried to turn, but the space around him became smaller and smaller until he couldn't move. He whinnied in terror and tried to kick out with his front legs, but to no avail.

Mandy had watched him helplessly. Then, when she couldn't bear his desperation any longer, she'd shouted out and woken herself up.

While the dream replayed itself in her mind, she found herself also remembering her nightmare after the trip to the mine. The sound of the frantic whinnying in that dream had stayed with her for days. Were the two dreams about the same pony? And if so, who was he? Was there something she was supposed to learn from the nightmares? Or was she making something out of nothing?

She remembered what her grandad had told her once when she'd woken up from a bad dream. He'd said that dreams were just the brain's way of sweeping out all the bits and pieces that were cluttering it up. "A kind of spring cleaning," he'd explained. Perhaps her nightmares were because of all the sad things she'd learned about pit ponies?

Mandy switched off the lamp, then lay down and pulled her comforter cozily around her. She decided to shut out the terrifying images and sounds of the nightmares by concentrating on the happy ponies she'd seen at Sunfield. She thought of Flame. Instantly, a vision of the handsome pony glowing in the sunshine came to her. She smiled as she remembered the intelligent way he'd looked at her. Then she drifted off to sleep again.

"You look exhausted," said Dr. Emily when Mandy joined her parents for breakfast in the morning. "Didn't you sleep well?"

"Not really," said Mandy. "I had another bad dream." She helped herself to a glass of orange juice, then flipped through the magazine section of the Sunday newspaper.

"Good thing it's Sunday," said Dr. Adam, buttering a slice of toast. "I don't think you'd cope too well with school today. Could you pass me the marmalade, please?"

Mandy handed him the jar. "I'll be okay, Dad. I don't feel too bad. It's just that the dream was a little scary."

She described what had happened.

"It sounds to me as if you're dwelling on the pit ponies just a little too much," said Dr. Emily, lifting a poached egg out of a pan of boiling water and putting it on Mandy's plate. "Maybe you should get outside and have some fun today. Think about something else for a change."

"I can't really do that," explained Mandy. She slid a piece of toast under the egg. "I have to work on my project today. It's got to be in on Wednesday and I've still got tons to do."

"Can't you do it tomorrow? You'll be home, won't you?" asked Dr. Emily. "Isn't it a teacher-training day?"

"Yes, but I still have to sort through all the information I've got and decide exactly how I'm going to do the project. Tomorrow, I'll start putting it all together," said Mandy. She cut into the egg and the yolk oozed onto the toast. "This is delicious. Thanks, Mom," she said.

"I've got an idea," said Dr. Adam. "Why don't you spend the morning working? Then after lunch we'll all go for a walk along the river."

"That sounds good," said Dr. Emily. "We'll take a picnic with us." She pulled her long red hair into a ponytail, then rolled up her sleeves to wash the dishes. "I'll even bake a cake!"

"Wonders will never cease!" teased Dr. Adam. "We'd better jump at the offer, Mandy. Who knows when Mom will repeat it?"

"Okay." Mandy grinned. She swallowed her last mouthful of egg, then pushed her chair back. "I'm just going to check on the animals."

Mandy liked to get involved in the running of Animal Ark as much as she could. She often helped out when the clinic was busy. Then, there were also her regular duties, such as feeding the animals that were recovering from illnesses or operations and cleaning out their cages. Hardly a day went by when she didn't help out with the animals — no matter how busy she was.

There were four animals in the residential unit that day — two cats that had been in a fight, a boxer puppy who had come in the previous evening with a broken leg, and a goat that had eaten some rat poison.

Mandy fed them all, gave them fresh water, and made sure they were clean and comfortable. Then she petted each one in turn, saying, "I'll be back later."

The puppy whined when he saw Mandy walking away.

"Don't cry, Punch," she said, returning to him and pushing her hand through the bars of the cage. "You'll be going home very soon." She massaged his neck gently until he relaxed, then stood up to sneak away. The puppy immediately started to whine again.

"Oh, Punch, I've *got* to go," Mandy said. She almost couldn't bear the look on his squashed-up little face.

How was she going to get away without him noticing? Punch whimpered and pawed at the gate. Mandy sighed. If only he'd stop looking so pitiful!

And then, something very strange happened. The puppy's eyes seemed to become the eyes she'd seen in the tunnel and it was as if his whining turned into the desperate neighing she'd heard in her dreams.

Mandy took a step back in astonishment and blinked. In that split second, the eyes returned to normal and the whining no longer sounded like neighing.

"That was strange," Mandy said aloud.

Punch wagged his stubby little tail and then, to Mandy's surprise, settled down and closed his eyes. She tiptoed out of the room, trying to make sense of the peculiar incident. It must have been her imagination again — especially after such vivid dreams.

She climbed the twisting staircase to her bedroom. Her mom was probably right. She should try to stop thinking about pit ponies for a while. Then she groaned, remembering all the work she still had to do on her project.

For the next few hours Mandy sat at her desk, sorting through the information she'd gathered so far. She wasn't sure whether to focus on the Amberton ponies or if her project should cover pit ponies in general. She found herself wishing that Ms. Potter hadn't told them to do a project. A short presentation about what they'd done at the museum would have been easier — and quicker!

It was slow going and Mandy struggled to concentrate. The nightmare had affected her more deeply than she'd thought. Images of the distressed pony from her dream kept forcing themselves to the front of her mind and she felt a restless anxiety in the pit of her stomach.

Finally, she slammed down her pen. "It's no use!" she exclaimed in frustration. "I'm getting nowhere!"

She put her work away and went downstairs to the kitchen, where she helped her mom pack the picnic.

It was a crisp, clear afternoon and the river sparkled in the sunlight as it tumbled and swirled over the rocks lying hidden beneath its surface. A family of mallards swam upstream, battling against the strong current.

"Aren't they funny?" laughed Mandy. "You'd think they'd swim with the current!"

"Perhaps they need to go up the river," suggested Dr. Adam.

"They could always walk along the bank," suggested his wife.

"I don't think so!" cried Mandy as a large and very wet black dog came hurtling along the bank toward them. "No, Blackie. Stay there!" she shouted.

But Blackie ignored Mandy's plea. He ran up to her, then stopped abruptly at her feet and shook himself vigorously, showering her with water.

"You bad boy!" Mandy scolded, laughing in spite of herself. The dog looked up and wagged his tail happily.

"Do you know, I think he's laughing at me," Mandy said to her parents. "How can you be angry with a dog that does that?" She looked around. "I wonder where James is."

Hearing the name of his master, Blackie turned and charged off, almost bumping into James, who was coming around a bend a few yards downstream.

"Sorry," said James.

Mandy smiled. James knew his dog very well! He didn't even have to ask why his friend was soaking wet. "It's okay," she laughed. "The water didn't get through my jacket. And, anyway, it's nice to get such a warm greeting."

"More like a cold one, if you ask me!" Dr. Adam laughed. Then he turned to James. "You're just in time. We're about to eat."

They found a good spot on the pebbly riverbank for their picnic and started eating the sandwiches, cake, and fruit that Mandy and Dr. Emily had packed.

"How's your project going?" James asked Mandy, helping himself to a slice of Dr. Emily's sponge cake.

"I've almost finished mine. I just need to do some drawings of the tunnel system at Amberton."

"Lucky you!" Mandy grumbled. "I've hardly started." She told him about her nightmare. "It's all I can think about. I haven't even really decided what to do my project on."

"But I thought you were going to report on pit ponies," said James, sounding surprised.

"Yes, but I don't know whether I should concentrate on the ponies that worked at Amberton — especially now that we've met a few of them."

"Why not?" asked James. "It sounds like a good idea."

"Yes, but I don't think I've got enough information on them," said Mandy, giving a small wedge of cheese to Blackie. The black Labrador was exhausted after splashing around in the river and now lay quietly beside her.

"Didn't you see any information about the ponies at the museum?" asked Dr. Emily. She opened the thermos flask and poured out some lemonade.

"Yes — a whole gallery of photographs," Mandy told her. "But we didn't have time to go through it all. I wish we could go back there."

Dr. Adam stretched over and took a cup of lemonade. "Thanks, honey," he said. He took a few gulps, then put the cup on a rock and said, "I think you *should* go back."

Mandy looked at him quizzically. "When?"

"What about tomorrow?" replied her father. "You're not going to school and we have a very quiet morning scheduled. There are only a few animals coming in for checkups and vaccinations. As soon as we've seen them, and as long as there are no emergencies, we can leave for Amberton and be back in time for the evening clinic." He turned to Dr. Emily. "Does that sound like a good idea?"

"I think it's an excellent idea," said Dr. Emily, enthusiastically. "I'd love to go on the underground tour and see what it's like in the tunnels."

Dr. Adam looked taken aback. "You want to go underground!" he exclaimed.

His wife nodded. "Yes, I do," she said seriously.

"Hang on," said Dr. Adam, standing up and putting his hands on his hips. "Aren't you the same person who once refused to go into the Chamber of Horrors at the fair?"

"Yes, but that was different," protested Dr. Emily.

"It's different, all right," agreed James. "The mine is much scarier than the Chamber of Horrors!"

"Does that mean you won't be joining us?" teased Dr. Adam.

James laughed. "I'm not the one who sees and hears things in dark tunnels!" He glanced at Mandy and she wrinkled her nose at him.

"Maybe it'll be your turn to imagine things this time," she joked. She picked up a stick and threw it up the bank. Blackie jumped up and ran off to retrieve the stick.

"Imagine *what* things?" asked Dr. Emily.

"Oh, nothing." Mandy tried to sound casual. Her experience down in the mine seemed unbelievable in broad daylight. "It's just a little spooky down there, that's all."

Dr. Adam winked at his wife. "Are you still game to go?"

"Of course," she said firmly.

"Okay, so it's decided," said Dr. Adam, helping his wife to her feet. "We'll set off for Amberton at about ten in the morning."

Blackie came thundering back down the bank, the stick firmly grasped between his teeth. The sound of his paws on the firm ground jolted Mandy's memory. She had a sudden flashback to the eerie clopping sound that she'd heard in the tunnel. And in her mind, she saw once more the blazing eyes that had taken her breath away. A shudder ran through her whole body.

Surprised that she still felt a little spooked, Mandy decided that it was time to pull herself together. Taking the stick from Blackie, she threw it along the bank. James's lively dog hurtled after the stick and Mandy trudged after him.

Six

"It was so real! I was sure that if I reached out, I'd be able to touch him," Mandy told James on their way to the Amberton Mine the next morning.

"What did he look like?" asked James, wiping the condensation off the window on his side of the Land Rover.

"The same as in the last dream — a chestnut Shetland — but this time, he was so close to me, I could feel his hot breath on my neck," said Mandy.

James looked at her in disbelief. "Feel his breath! But you were dreaming, Mandy!"

"I know. But honestly, James, it felt like it was real,"

Mandy explained. She knew that if she shut her eyes now, she'd get a very clear picture of the pony. It was as if he were carved forever in her mind.

"So what happened in *this* nightmare?" asked James.

Mandy sighed and looked out of her window. The fields and valleys rushed by in a gray, misty blur. Every now and then, she could see horses sheltering under trees from the driving rain and icy wind. Some of them looked really miserable — almost as miserable as the pony in her latest nightmare.

"What happened?" repeated James, looking concerned.

"It was almost the same as the last two dreams," said Mandy, still staring out of her window. She didn't want to talk about the dream anymore. It just churned her up inside. But even though it was the same dream, with the same pony, it *had* been different. This time, instead of watching him from a distance, Mandy had been right next to him. This time she had not only seen but had also *felt* his desperation. It was as if they shared a feeling of terror while the space folded in around them.

She closed her eyes and the blackness behind her eyelids was instantly filled with the features of the terrified Shetland — the flared nostrils, eyes wide with fear, the foam around his mouth. In the dream, she'd wanted to turn and run but something had stopped her.

She couldn't leave the pony. She knew that they had to face the terror together.

"How did it end?" asked James.

Mandy shook herself. "Um, I'm not sure. I don't think it did end. I think it just sort of faded away. Or maybe I woke up before the end. I don't know," she sighed.

"I wonder if bad dreams ever have endings?" pondered Dr. Emily, looking over her shoulder at Mandy and James. "I've never had one that ended definitely — I'm always trying to get away from something terrible, but I'm frozen solid!"

Suddenly, Dr. Adam braked sharply. "Oops, nearly missed the turn in all this mist," he said. He swung the Land Rover down a road to the right.

There were only two other cars and a workman's van in the parking lot outside the museum building. Both cars had bumper stickers that read AMBERTON MINING MUSEUM — WE GO THE EXTRA MILE.

"Must be staff cars," said Dr. Adam, as they walked over to the main building.

Inside the museum, they found Lisa sitting behind the information desk, wearing a big winter coat. She smiled warmly at them. "Hi there. I was wondering if anyone would come to the mine in this awful weather." She looked closely at Mandy and James. "Don't I recognize you two? Didn't you come with the school group last week?"

Mandy nodded, and then explained why they'd returned.

"Well, it looks like you have the whole place to yourselves today. You can spend as much time as you like researching your project. Please ask if there's anything I can help you with," said Lisa. "And, of course, Mr. Etherington can tell you just about anything you want to know about the ponies."

Dr. Adam pulled his wallet out of his pocket to pay for the admission fees. "Will you give an underground tour for such a small group?"

"Certainly," Lisa reassured him. "Arthur — the guide — can take you down whenever you like." She handed him the release forms, then said, "I must apologize about the cold in here. We had a power outage earlier this morning. It lasted only ten minutes, but it's affected the heating system. Our electricians are looking into it, so we hope it'll be fixed soon."

Mandy wrapped her arms closely around herself. No wonder she was shivering so much!

"What caused the power failure?" asked James.

Lisa shrugged her shoulders. "We don't know. It could have been the weather — there was a raging storm at the time — but apparently the town of Amberton didn't get cut off and they're on the same grid as us. The electricians have checked all of our systems here but haven't been able to find the problem yet. So, who knows! It's just one of those mysteries."

James looked at Mandy and winked.

Mandy made a face. But she couldn't help remembering how her headlamp had also gone out briefly for no real reason, when she and James were in the side tunnel the other day.

She tried to ignore a growing feeling of unease. But there was nothing she could put her finger on. Was it just the gloomy weather? Or was she worried that she might have the same creepy experience as the last time she'd been down in the mine? And then there was the incident with Christie. Maybe she was afraid she'd also faint. After all, it *was* very dark and stuffy underground.

Arthur was sitting in an easy chair reading the *Amberton Town Gazette* in the office next to the elevator shaft. Wafts of hot air blew out from a small space heater, making the temperature inside the office very different from the chilly conditions elsewhere. As on their previous visit, Arthur handed each of them a safety helmet before they stepped into the big elevator.

Mandy braced herself for the mile-and-a-quarter

plunge into the dark abyss. Even though she knew what to expect, she couldn't brush aside a small tingling feeling in the pit of her stomach as Arthur dragged the gate shut with a loud clang.

The old miner pushed up a big lever on one of the walls of the elevator. There was the familiar jerking movement they'd experienced on their first trip, then the metal cage plummeted down the cold, murky shaft to the hostile depths of the earth below.

"Well, that was quite breathtaking," Dr. Emily remarked once the elevator had hit hard ground. "I hadn't imagined it would be so dark or that we'd drop so quickly."

The main heading seemed gloomier than before. Mandy reasoned that it was because there were fewer headlamps in the tunnel today — only five this time as opposed to the thirty or so on the school tour.

Arthur led them down the passage, repeating the talk he'd given the school group a few days earlier. "Amberton is a typical deep shaft mine. This means that the access passages run straight down from the surface to the coal seam."

"So there's more than one way into the mine?" asked Dr. Adam.

"Yes. The way we've just come is how all the miners

used to get into and out of the mine. And then there's the coal-removal passage, which is about fifty yards farther along," Arthur explained.

"Does this mine have sloping passages?" asked James, who was just behind Arthur.

Arthur sounded a little surprised by James's question. "Yes, we *do* have a passage dug on a slant. It's farther away, where there used to be a coal seam under a hill. A slanting passage is the best way to reach coal in that position. Have you been reading up on tunneling?"

James told him about his project. "I looked up the Amberton Museum web site on the Internet last night. There's a page all about the different types of tunnels in the mine. There's even a map that shows all the smaller side tunnels and the emergency passages. I've got a printout with me."

Arthur seemed impressed but also a little puzzled. "Well, I know nothing about all this newfangled computer stuff but I do know about tunnels. And, because you're a small group, what I can do — and your computer can't — is take you down one of the emergency tunnels. That way you can experience for real what it was like for miners years ago."

"That should be interesting," said Dr. Adam.

James nudged Mandy and she grinned, then lifted a finger to her lips. They'd better not let on that they'd already been along one of the smaller passages — on their own!

They had reached the section where the main heading forked. As before, Arthur led them down the passageway to the right. After a few minutes he stopped. "The emergency passage is through here." He shone his headlamp against the wall, revealing a small timber-framed hole that had been cut out of the rock.

Mandy put a hand to her mouth and stifled a gasp. It was the same hole that she and James had gone through on the day of the school trip. The hole that led to the echoing passage — the passage that, if she was honest with herself, she was still sure hid a secret. But was she brave enough to find out what it was? Part of her wanted to turn and head back to the elevator and return to the normal world above. But another part was determined to face whatever the passage might be hiding.

"It looks a little like an entrance to a cave," remarked Dr. Adam from the back of the line. He'd brought a flashlight with him and was aiming the beam at the hole, which suddenly looked very small. "It's going to be a bit of a tight squeeze for me," he said.

"Maybe we shouldn't go in," said Mandy, giving in for a moment to a feeling of apprehension about the passageway.

"I'm sure if I hold by breath, I'll fit through," her father answered, chuckling.

"But it looks very narrow in there, Dad," argued Mandy.

"That's all right. We're not going all the way, are we, Arthur?" asked Dr. Adam.

"No — just far enough for you to get a sense of what it was like to work in such conditions," said Arthur. "Mandy's right — it does get very cramped after a while. Of course, we *can* go right through if you want to see where it ends up."

"No, thanks," muttered Dr. Emily. "Just getting the idea of it will be enough for me!"

One by one they crawled through the gap into the unlit and airless space beyond. Even though she'd felt anxious a few moments before, Mandy's heart now raced with excitement. Could there really be something extraordinary in that tunnel? And would she see it again?

"Ouch!" cried Dr. Adam, struggling through the hole. *"Ouch! Ouch! Ouch!"* echoed his voice.

James laughed. "I think the echo's the best thing about the tunnel, don't you, Mandy?" His laughter bounced around them as they filed along the passage.

"So far," agreed Mandy, and she grinned as her own voice came tumbling back at her.

"Can you switch on your headlamp, Mandy?" asked Arthur after a while, glancing over his shoulder.

Mandy was confused. She hadn't switched it off. She flicked the switch but nothing happened. "The bulb must have gone out," she said.

"It can't have," said Arthur. "I put new bulbs in all of these helmets only yesterday."

Again, Mandy fiddled with the switch, but nothing happened. Then she looked behind her and noticed that her mom's lamp had also gone out. She felt a sense of foreboding. Something definitely wasn't right.

"Let's go back," she said, trying to sound calm. She had hardly finished speaking when they were suddenly plunged into total darkness. The rest of the headlamps had been extinguished in one swoop like candles blown out by a strong gust of wind.

Dr. Emily gasped.

"Don't worry," came Arthur's soothing voice. "I've got my flashlight."

There was a rustling sound followed by a clicking noise, then a sudden "Uh-oh!" and Mandy realized that the flashlight had also failed. She tried to take a breath, but the stale and clammy air stuck in her throat.

"Keep calm, everyone," Arthur said from the front of the group. "We'll just turn and make our way back to the entrance. We're not far from the main heading — you'll even see the light ahead of us."

In spite of Arthur's reassuring tone, Mandy was convinced that something strange was happening. First the power in the museum had gone off for no reason and now this.

The darkness pressed in on her like a sinister force and her mouth felt dry. What explanation could there be for five lamps and a flashlight all going out at the same time?

They began to maneuver themselves around in the narrow space. Mandy's fingers scraped against the jagged wall.

"Are you okay?" whispered James, after accidentally bumping into her.

"Uh-huh," she said, taking a step forward. "I just scraped my —" She stopped abruptly. There was a new sound in the tunnel. A sound that rose distinctly above the noise of their awkward movements.

"What's wrong?" asked James, bumping into her again.

"Shh," she whispered. She waited, her senses made acute by the silent darkness. And then she heard it again. A faint, lonely whinnying that came from deep within the tunnel.

"Anything the matter?" Arthur's low voice rumbled in the gloom behind them as he found his way blocked by James.

"I don't know." Mandy waited and listened again. The forlorn sound rose up to her from the hidden depths of the earth.

"Listen," she said to the others. "Can you hear that?" The neighing had grown louder and more urgent.

"Yes," breathed James in astonishment. "It sounds like a horse."

"What are you two talking about?" Dr. Emily had stopped just ahead of Mandy. She reached back into the darkness and caught hold of Mandy's sleeve.

Dr. Adam had also stopped to find out what was happening. Mandy could just make out his form against the faint light filtering through the entrance to the passage. He took a few steps back until he was part of the group. They all listened for the sound that Mandy had heard. "What am I missing?" he asked.

"Some wild imaginings!" Dr. Emily chuckled. "I can't hear anything strange, Mandy."

"But *I* heard it," insisted James.

"Listen — there it is again!" Mandy was surprised that only she and James could hear the urgent whinnying. It seemed to fill the tunnel around them.

"Perhaps you're hearing the wind whistling down the shaft and along the passages," Arthur suggested. "Come on — let's get out of here."

Mandy was no longer in a hurry to leave the narrow passage. She glanced over her shoulder into the blackness, then saw something that made her go cold. "Wait!" she cried. "Look there — back down the tunnel!"

Out of the darkness flickered a tiny bright light. Mandy strained her eyes, trying to make out what it was. It grew brighter and bigger. It was coming toward them! Then Mandy saw that there were two lights. She felt the hair on the back of her neck stand up. They weren't lights at all. They were eyes. The very same ones she'd seen here before!

James, who had also turned to look behind him, whispered softly, "Eyes!" He breathed in amazement. "So you *were* right the other day, Mandy. It wasn't just a reflection — or your imagination."

Dr. Emily touched Mandy's sleeve. "I think that's enough of this little joke now," she said firmly. "We're the only ones down here and if you think you can scare me with talk of strange noises and things —"

A sudden loud and heavy thud farther up the passage toward the entrance stopped Dr. Emily and made everyone jump. Mandy looked around. The faint light that had shone through the entrance to the passage had gone out. It was darker than ever. *Not another power outage*, thought Mandy.

"What was that?" Dr. Adam sounded concerned.

"I don't know," came Arthur's voice. "Can you see anything ahead of you?"

"Nothing," replied Dr. Adam. "But I'll feel my way and see what I can find." Mandy heard him shuffling toward the tunnel entrance. When he spoke again a few seconds later, his voice was brittle. "I can feel a big rock in front of me. I don't think I can get past it!"

Mandy's heart skipped a beat. What was going on down here?

"Does that mean we're blocked in?" Dr. Emily asked slowly.

"Just a second," said Arthur. "I'll see if I can get there to have a look myself. Sorry," he apologized as he squeezed past Mandy, causing her to be pushed up against the rough wall.

"Do you think your mom's right? Are we blocked in?" James asked Mandy in a low voice.

"Not really — remember, this is an emergency exit," Mandy reminded him, trying not to sound worried. If only they had some light.

She looked past James into the dark space beyond, trying to make sense of everything that was happening to them. There was no longer any sign of the mysterious eyes. She frowned. Even the darkness seemed to be getting thicker just ahead of them. Mandy wondered if it was a wall. She blinked hard.

Then, out of the solid darkness, a shape began to emerge. It was the unmistakable shape of a small colt! "It's a pony," she whispered, forgetting for a moment the crisis at the entrance to the passage.

"Yikes!" exclaimed James. "It is! How did *he* get here?"

A shimmering phosphorescence radiated from the colt that stood proudly before them. And in the glow, Mandy could see that it was a Shetland pony. A chestnut Shetland pony.

Seven

"Who *are* you? What are you doing down here?" Mandy mouthed the questions but no sound came from her lips. The vision of the pony had stunned her. Yet it was no hallucination. James could see him, too.

"Where did he come from?" James repeated.

At the same time, Arthur called out that a large rock was in fact blocking the way to the entrance. "We might have disturbed the support frame when we climbed through," he explained, "which could have dislodged the rock and made it fall. I can't think what else might have caused it. I mean, there's been no shaking or rumbling down here so we're probably not in any danger.

Lucky we'd stopped for a little while, though — otherwise someone might have gotten hurt or even . . ." He didn't continue.

"So that means we'll have to get out at the other end?" asked Dr. Adam.

"I'm afraid so," said Arthur. "But it'll be fine — just a little tight in places. I'll lead the way again."

A heaving noise sounded in the roof above them. Instantly, Arthur yelled out, "I don't like the sound of that! Don't wait for me up ahead — just get started, and move as fast as you can!"

"Hurry, Mandy!" Dr. Emily prodded her in the back and Mandy started to move as quickly as she could in the cramped space. The sound of everyone's boots pounding on the rough ground echoed around her and, every now and then, she found herself bumping into James, who was just ahead of her. She could hear her mother's breathing several feet behind her and she realized that she and James were moving a lot faster than the adults. She pushed a strand of hair out of her face. It was damp with perspiration. Was that just because of the heat down here or was it from fear?

The alarming noise stopped but Arthur urged them to get to the other end fast. "Just in case the disturbance was bigger than I thought," he shouted from the back.

Then he added reassuringly, "The tunnel's not very long — we should be out of here in a few minutes."

Ahead, Mandy could still see the outline of the pony who was standing quietly watching them. When she and James had almost reached him he turned sideways and flexed his neck, then opened his mouth in a silent whinny.

"He's trying to tell us something," Mandy said breathlessly to James.

"I hope it's that we're not in danger," answered James, and Mandy could hear the tension in his voice.

The pony snorted. He struck the ground a few times with his hooves, then spun around and stared straight at Mandy. She gasped. His bright eyes seemed to draw her in like a magnet. It was as if she was a prisoner of his gaze. And it was a gaze she'd felt before. For a brief moment, she was back at the Sunfield Pony Sanctuary. *Like Flame!* she said to herself. *His stare is exactly like Flame's!*

Bewildered by the strange coincidence, Mandy almost lost her balance as she scrambled over the uneven ground. She pushed her hands against the walls on either side to steady herself and, in that moment, the pony vanished.

"Hey!" exclaimed James. "Where did he go?"

But before Mandy could speak, the tunnel was suddenly lit up by a soft yellow light.

"Oh!" gasped everyone in surprise. Their headlamps were working again!

"Well, I never . . ." muttered Arthur from the back.

The beams from their lamps broke the darkness around them and, once Mandy's eyes became adjusted to the light, she could see that the tunnel was much smaller than at the beginning.

Everyone stopped and looked at one another as if to take stock of their situation. Apart from the sound of their rapid breathing, there was complete silence.

"This is so weird!" James said, shaking his head, then pushing his messy hair off his forehead.

"Uh-huh. It's almost uncanny," murmured Dr. Emily.

"I must say, I've never experienced anything like it," Arthur said.

"Well, I don't think we'll come up with any answers down here," said Dr. Adam. "And I think that the sooner we get out of this place, the better."

The group pressed on again with James still in the lead. The tunnel was now so narrow that Mandy had to keep her elbows tucked closely by her sides to stop them from being scraped by the walls. She looked up and her headlamp shone against the roof, which was now only just above her. She'd have to duck down if it got any lower.

She glanced back over her shoulder and saw that her parents and Arthur were almost bent over. Dr. Adam, being the largest of the three, filled the space around him.

"If it gets much tighter, I won't be able to go on," he grunted.

But the tunnel did get tighter and the roof lower. Mandy looked back again and saw with alarm that her father was almost on his stomach. What if it got too narrow for him?

"Mandy! Look!" James blurted out, breaking into Mandy's concerned thoughts.

In front of them, standing silhouetted against a dimly lit background, was the colt. He whinnied softly, then struck the ground with his hooves over and over again.

"What do you want?" breathed Mandy.

But the pony gave away no clues about himself. He shook his head vigorously, then silently disappeared once more. And in the place where he'd been standing, Mandy saw an illuminated arched hole. It was the end of the emergency tunnel.

"We've made it!" exclaimed James triumphantly.

Mandy tapped him on the shoulder. "Good job,

leader," she laughed. She felt the tension lifting from her as she ran after him through the small gap into the airier space of the bigger tunnel beyond. It was great to be able to stand up straight again and not to feel closed in on all sides. She looked around to see if there was any sign of the colt. But there was no trace of him.

"Phew! That's better." Dr. Adam emerged through the gap behind Dr. Emily and stretched and dusted himself off. "Now what?"

"We're in the tunnel that forks off to the left of the main heading," Arthur explained, climbing through the hole. "If we work our way back we'll reach the elevator. Would you like to rest first?"

"Good idea," said Dr. Adam. "I feel as if I've been on some kind of obstacle course!" He leaned against the wall, breathing deeply.

Mandy didn't want to rest. She wanted to know what had happened to the colt. He had to be somewhere close by. She could see that James was also puzzled by his disappearance. He paced back and forth, fidgeting with his glasses and occasionally kicking idly at the rocky ground. Then he stopped and knelt down, angling his head as if trying to look at something with his head-lamp.

"What is it?" asked Mandy, going over to him.

"A hoofprint, I think," he answered.

Mandy examined the ground. There was a faint horseshoe-shaped impression in the surface where James was pointing. Then she noticed another one close by. She shone her beam along the ground and saw a line of hoofprints going up the tunnel. Were they the prints of the mysterious colt?

"Let's see where they go," said James, standing up but bending his head so that his lamp lit up the trail.

The two set off down the passage.

"Where are you going?" called Dr. Emily.

"We're just going a little closer toward the shaft," explained Mandy.

"After some phantom horse, I suppose!" Dr. Adam said, laughing. "Don't get too far in front of us."

Mandy sighed with frustration. Why hadn't the adults been able to see or hear the pony?

The two friends followed the prints for several yards until, near a bend in the passage, the trail stopped abruptly.

"Oh well, that's the end of that," said Mandy. "Maybe they're not hoofprints at all — they just look like them."

"I suppose it was a bit of a wild-horse chase." James grinned.

Mandy laughed and looked up. Her smile faded instantly for, standing in front of her — so close that she could have reached out and touched his forehead —

was the chestnut pony. Next to her, James sucked in his breath, then stretched his hand toward the little Shetland.

The pony bucked his head and snorted loudly, then whirled around and trotted up the passage. Mandy's headlamp lit up his face for a split second before he charged off. But in that brief moment she caught sight of his expression. It was the same as the look of terror of the pony in her dreams!

"He is trying to tell us something," Mandy insisted. "I *know* he is."

"Maybe he wants us to follow him," said James, scrambling off after the colt.

The pony had rounded the bend and was out of sight but Mandy could hear his hooves clattering on the hard ground. "I think you're right," she said.

She couldn't understand why, but she had begun to feel a strong sense of urgency. She set off behind James, calling back over her shoulder, "Mom, Dad, Arthur — you've got to come now. We have to get to the elevator quickly!"

She could hear that the pony was now galloping so she quickened her own pace.

"Wait, Mandy," Dr. Emily shouted from behind. "Not so fast!"

"Hurry!" Mandy cried out, ignoring her mom's plea.

Mandy and James reached the point where the two tunnels merged into the main heading.

"We're almost back at the shaft," James reminded Mandy.

Out of the corner of her eye, Mandy saw James suddenly stumble and trip and fall to the ground. His glasses flew off, landing in front of Mandy. She grabbed them and handed them back to him as he got back up on his feet.

"Now maybe you'll slow down!" said Dr. Emily firmly as she and Dr. Adam and Arthur caught up with them.

"Yes," agreed Arthur. "I've never known anyone who could run so fast in a tunnel. Not since . . ."

A distant noise interrupted him. From deep in the earth came an ominous rumbling.

"Quickly!" shouted Arthur. "Head for the shaft!"

"What's happening?" cried Dr. Emily just as the earth began to tremble and shake beneath them.

"An earthquake!" yelled Arthur. "Run!"

The rumbling noise intensified and was accompanied by loud thuds, while in the tunnel the lamps on the walls began to flicker. Ahead of them, the pony whinnied frantically.

Mandy dashed along the tunnel, her heart pounding in her chest. In front of her she could see the pony again. He had stopped and seemed to be waiting for them to catch up. They were only a few feet away from him when Mandy realized that he was standing in front of the cage. He kicked at the gate and it slid open, then he took a few steps to the side.

"He's opened the elevator for us!" exclaimed James.

"Go on in, little pony," urged Mandy, running the last few feet to the elevator.

The earth shook violently beneath her. She glanced over her shoulder and saw that the others were hot on her heels. Dr. Emily staggered and fell against Dr. Adam, who caught hold of her arm and steadied her.

There was another lurch just as Mandy reached the elevator door and, in that moment, the pony melted away into the darkness.

Mandy blinked then stared hard at the spot where he'd been standing. Perhaps he'd moved into a shadow. But there wasn't even a hint of his presence. It was as if he'd never been there in the first place.

The others leaped into the cage behind Mandy and James, and Arthur pulled the gate shut. "I hope the lever is working," he mumbled apprehensively.

They watched anxiously as the miner took hold of the controls. There was a shudder and a creak but the elevator stayed on the ground.

"Come on! Move!" growled Arthur, pushing up the lever again.

Mandy crossed her fingers and willed the elevator to move. But even as she stood waiting nervously for the machinery to begin hauling them away from danger, a strange calm descended on her. And, with the calm came a dazzling vision of the colt. Instead of the wild expression on his face, he now wore a look of complete joy. Then he closed his eyes and a split second later, the vision faded.

Dr. Adam had put his arm around Mandy's shoulders. In a soothing tone he said, "Don't worry, Mandy. We'll get out of here."

Calmly, she looked up at her father. "I'm not worried. I know we're going to be okay." Then she smiled at James. "We had a good leader."

"Oh, yes. Thanks, James, for running ahead," said Dr. Adam.

James shrugged his shoulders. "It wasn't me. . . ." he began just as there was another jolt and a shudder and the elevator began to move slowly upward.

They stood in silence while the big steel cage carried them up the icy shaft to safety. But Mandy didn't feel the cold wind that hovered and howled in the shaft. A warm breeze tickled the back of her neck like the breath of a friendly pony.

Eight

At the surface, the gate was swiftly drawn aside and daylight flooded into the elevator. It was one of the most welcome sights Mandy had ever seen. She stepped out into the cold, fresh air to find a group of worried-looking people waiting for them.

Lisa was among the group. "Are you all okay? Did everyone get out?" she asked frantically. When she realized that no one was missing or hurt, she sighed with relief. "Phew. Thank goodness you're all right."

She led them to the restaurant where blankets and pots of hot chocolate were waiting for them.

"Really, I'm fine," James protested as Lisa draped a blanket around him.

Mandy thought that he looked a little dazed but she knew that he'd never admit it. She grinned as he squirmed and shook off the blanket but gratefully accepted the hot chocolate that was poured for him.

Mandy coughed to clear her throat of coal dust. She took a sip of her drink and looked across the table at her parents. Dr. Emily's red hair fell around her pale face. She smiled weakly at Mandy. "That was a close call," she said.

Mandy nodded. "But we did have help."

"Oh, yes, the pony!" exclaimed James. "I wonder what happened to the pony."

"Pony?" Lisa sounded puzzled.

"The pony down in the mine," Mandy explained.

Lisa frowned, then shot a glance at Arthur, who shook his head and shrugged his shoulders.

"I expect you were just a little confused by all the noise and tremors down there," said Lisa. "Shock can cause all sorts of reactions."

"I'm not in shock," Mandy insisted, "and there *was* a pony down there. James and I both saw it. It was a chestnut Shetland pony. We even followed it along the tunnel."

Lisa smiled at Mandy and James. "Well, if you say you saw a pony, then you must have seen one. But the important thing is that you're all safe." She went on to tell them that it was the first time anything dangerous had happened since the museum had been opened to the public. "And it was just so sudden — we had no warning at all."

"But we did," declared Mandy. She turned to James and said meaningfully, "The pony warned us, didn't he?"

"Uh-huh," said James. "When we saw him, we knew that something was wrong."

Arthur winked at Dr. Adam. "It would have helped if he'd warned *me*," he said and chuckled. Then he stood up, explaining that he'd have to get a team together to go down and check the extent of the damage. "It's the first time in many years we've had to organize a search party," he said gravely.

Mandy wanted to ask him to look for the colt, but she could guess that he wouldn't take her seriously. Instead, she asked when the team would be going down in the mine. She felt that the sooner they went, the better their chance of finding the pony.

"We'll set off just as soon as we're sure that there are no more aftershocks," Arthur said. "I think we'll probably be ready to go before lunch. We'll just carry out a quick structural check today, so we won't be very long. If you want to wait until we resurface, I'll be able to let you know how it went."

"I think we can wait a while," said Dr. Adam. "I don't feel up to driving at the moment and I'd like to hear all the details."

After Arthur left, Lisa offered to make them lunch. "How about some homemade soup?" she asked.

"Mmm, sounds good," said Dr. Adam, smiling gratefully.

"I'll talk it over with the chef." She walked toward the kitchen door, then stopped and turned. "Oh, by the way, the heat's on again," Lisa said. "It just suddenly started working at about the same time you were coming up in the elevator. It should start warming up in here any minute now."

Mandy went across to a window that overlooked the courtyard where the large mining machines were displayed. It was still very wet and misty outside, the rain dripping steadily off the huge pieces of equipment.

James came over to her. "I wish someone would believe us about the pony," he said, leaning on the windowsill and looking out into the yard. "But I guess it does sound a bit crazy."

"I know," Mandy agreed. "If I hadn't seen it with my own eyes, I'd agree with you."

"Hey, look. Isn't that Mr. Etherington?" James pointed toward a man sloshing through the puddles in the courtyard toward the blacksmith's yard.

"It looks like him," said Mandy. "Oh, no! I nearly forgot!" Seeing the blacksmith made her suddenly remember why they'd come back to the museum in the first place. In all the drama of their underground escape, she'd forgotten about her project! "Let's go and have a look at the pony gallery while we're waiting for lunch," she said urgently.

Dr. Adam and Dr. Emily chose not to go with Mandy and James. "I'd rather stay here where it's warm and dry," said Dr. Adam, flipping through a book on the museum.

The two friends went out to the courtyard, then darted through the rain to the yard.

Mr. Etherington had lit a roaring fire and was warming his hands in front of it. "This is the best place to be when the weather's so bad," he said with a smile when he saw Mandy and James coming toward him.

The heat radiated powerfully from the furnace, penetrating Mandy's jacket and making her feel uncomfortably hot. It reminded her of how sweltering it had been underground. She took a few steps backward. "Do you mind if we look around the gallery again?" she asked.

"Be my guests," said Mr. Etherington. "But I'm afraid

that some of the photos are missing at the moment. The people at the pony sanctuary have borrowed them."

"Sunfield Pony Sanctuary?" asked Mandy.

"Yes," answered Mr. Etherington. "They want to make a brochure or something about the place. They promised to return them today."

"Let's hope they bring them back before we leave," said James. He picked up a lump of metal. "Is this what you use to make horseshoes, Mr. Etherington?"

The old blacksmith nodded. "It's iron. Would you like to try?"

"Yes, please!" James answered eagerly.

Mr. Etherington picked up a strong pair of metal tongs and held the lump of metal in the flames. After a while, the iron began to glow red hot. Mr. Etherington pulled it out of the fire and put it on an anvil before pounding it with a hammer. He then offered James a turn.

James took hold of the heavy hammer. He struck the metal with all his might but made no mark on it.

"I think you'd better put it back in the fire to soften the iron more," said the blacksmith and offered James the tongs.

While Mr. Etherington and James worked the lump of metal, Mandy wandered up the steps to the gallery. There was a blank section on one wall where photos

had been removed. A few pictures remained and Mandy studied them and the details about each pony, jotting down notes in the notebook she'd brought with her.

Even though she filled up several pages with useful facts, she wasn't really thinking about her work. Instead she was looking for something else — some information that would throw light on the mysterious pony they'd seen. Surely there must be some clues to his identity. She was quite sure that he belonged to the Amberton mine so she had expected to find at least a picture of him in the gallery.

But she found nothing. Feeling dissatisfied, Mandy walked back down the stairs and returned to James and Mr. Etherington, who were still busily hammering the metal into an arc.

"Did you find what you were looking for?" asked the man.

"Not really," replied Mandy. She pulled herself up onto the low wall that separated the forge from the rest of the yard and watched the blacksmith and his new apprentice.

"What are you looking for?" Mr. Etherington pulled the glowing metal out of the fire and held it still while James flattened it a little more with the hammer. "Are you looking for evidence of the pony you saw underground?" A kindly expression softened his lined, reddened face.

Mandy looked at him in surprise. Then she realized that James must have told him about the pony. "Do you believe us?" she asked.

Mr. Etherington lifted up the tongs and inspected his and James's handiwork. "We're getting there, James," he said, then turned to Mandy. "Who can say what others see? You know, sometimes I could swear that I hear ponies neighing and trotting in this very yard." He looked out from the forge and ran his eyes over the cobblestone yard. "But someone else will only hear the wind howling down the corridors and the crack of breaking branches in the trees."

"But he *was* real. We could have touched him. Isn't that right, James?" said Mandy.

James stopped hammering. Perspiration lined his forehead and he was breathing deeply. "Yes, and we even saw his hoofprints," he said solemnly.

"Well then — if you both agree he was real, that's all the evidence you need," said Mr. Etherington. He flicked the horseshoe out of the tongs. "I think that's good enough now," he told James. "We'll let it cool down."

"But I want to know who the pony is and what he's doing down there," insisted Mandy.

"And if he's all right," added James.

"There are some things in this life we can never know." The man's voice made Mandy think of a wise old owl. He turned his head to one side, listening attentively to something. "That's the sound of the elevator," he said after a moment. "The search team's coming back up."

"Great!" exclaimed James. "Now we'll find out what's really going on!"

Mr. Etherington doused the flames, as they hurried out of the yard and back to the restaurant. Mandy's heart had started to thud painfully. What if the colt hadn't survived?

Minutes later, when Arthur came through the restaurant doors, everyone looked up eagerly. His face was blackened with coal smudges and his overalls were covered with a fine layer of coal dust.

"It was definitely an earthquake," he said, sitting at the table next to James. "I checked the seismic equipment in the control room before we went down and it measured three on the Richter scale."

"Three!" James sounded dismayed. "We were lucky to get out alive."

"We were," agreed Arthur solemnly. "And contrary to what I first thought, it's not a pretty sight down there. We could only get to the first hundred feet or so."

"Is the whole tunnel system destroyed?" James said quietly.

"We can't say yet," Arthur answered. "But we think that the passages beyond the fork are blocked by tons of rock."

A new pang of fear gripped Mandy's heart. They'd been in far more danger than she'd imagined.

Arthur continued, "In all my years of mining, I've only

once seen damage like this — more than thirty years ago. That was caused by an earthquake, too."

"I remember that quake," Mr. Etherington said quietly. "A terrible tragedy."

Everyone seemed dazed by the news. Dr. Adam stared blankly at Arthur. He tugged at his beard, deep in thought, then at last he murmured, "It's probably just sheer luck that we got out in time."

"Probably," said Arthur solemnly. He reached into his pocket and drew out a dirty, creased sheet of paper.

"What's that?" asked Mandy.

"It's a map of the mine's tunnel system," explained Arthur, running a stubby finger across it. "Going by what we experienced in the tunnel, it's my guess that the rockfall started in this area." He pointed to the right-hand fork of the main heading. "Then it spread along the emergency tunnel and up the other main passage as far as the fork."

"If that is how it happened, then we were just ahead of the falling rocks," said Dr. Emily grimly. "If we'd slowed down or stopped any longer to rest, we might not have made it!" She shook her head and sighed.

"Well, we did make it — thanks to Mandy and James running ahead of us," said Dr. Adam. "Anyway, the main thing is that we're all sitting here together now."

"I know," murmured Dr. Emily. "But imagine if Mandy and James hadn't held us back when they thought they heard something in the emergency tunnel? We might have been caught in the first fall."

Mandy shuddered. Then, a new thought suddenly came to her. Almost like a cool breeze, it swept away the turmoil in her head, leaving her with a feeling of deep peace.

Mandy was certain that they'd never been in real danger. The colt had made sure of that.

Nine

Mandy didn't feel like eating. She halfheartedly sipped some of the soup that a waitress had brought them. Then she put down her spoon while her mind churned over the events in the tunnel.

The little colt had been so brave. But what had happened to him? Had he managed to find his way out? She remembered what Arthur had told them about the slope entrance to the mine. She nudged James, who was eating a crusty bread roll. The events down in the mine obviously hadn't ruined *his* appetite! "I wonder if the pony used the slope passage to get into the mine?"

James shrugged his shoulders while he swallowed a

mouthful of bread. "I dunno. But I hope so. At least then he'd have stood a chance of getting out again."

Overhearing them, Arthur leaned back in his chair and smiled. "Still talking about that pony?"

"I *know* there was a pony — a very brave one," insisted Mandy in frustration, "and he *must* have gotten into the mine somehow."

Arthur shook his head slowly. "Sorry to disappoint you, but there's no way a pony — or anyone else, for that matter — could go down the slope passage. It's been boarded up for years. Anyway, it doesn't lead into the main heading." He pointed to the slope tunnel on the map. "But one thing you've said is absolutely true," he added unexpectedly.

Mandy shot a surprised glance at James, who looked equally astounded by Arthur's comment.

"Ponies *can* be very brave. I've known some to stand quite calmly, refusing to budge because they've sensed that a rockfall is about to happen," Arthur explained.

James whistled softly. "Awesome!" he exclaimed. "Like a sixth sense?"

"That's what many of us who worked with the ponies believe." Mr. Etherington's grave tone made everyone stop eating and look at him inquiringly.

The blacksmith seemed to be lost in thought. For a

moment he sat quietly, staring into the distance, then he took a deep breath and shook himself. "There are many tales of ponies being very perceptive," he began. "There was the pony who stopped of his own accord when a miner's foot got caught under the wheels of a loaded car. The creature couldn't see what had happened but, somehow, he just knew. Otherwise, the miner would have lost his foot."

"That's incredible," commented Dr. Adam, slowly ladling more soup into his bowl. "I know that horses are intelligent, but that really makes you think."

"And if you want to know about real courage," continued the blacksmith, "there's the story of the time about a hundred years ago when a pony suddenly refused to go forward. When his handler pushed past him to investigate, he found a young boy sleeping on the ground some distance ahead — right in the path of the pony. If he'd gone on, the heavy cart he was dragging would have killed the boy."

Mandy's parents shook their heads in amazement. "That defies all reason," said Dr. Emily. "How did he know that the boy was there?"

As Mandy took in the remarkable story, a new idea began to form in her mind. Her project would include a special section that described how the instincts of the pit ponies had saved lives in the mine. "The miners must have been really grateful for the ponies' warnings," she said thoughtfully.

Mr. Etherington's response surprised her. "Sadly not," he said. "For instance, in the severe earthquake here about thirty years ago when the tunnels were blocked for weeks —"

At that moment, he was interrupted by the waitress who cleared away the plates.

"Thank you very much," said Dr. Emily, passing a soup bowl to the waitress. Then she looked at her watch. "Mr. Etherington, we've loved hearing these fascinating stories, but we really ought to get going now. We haven't got long before the afternoon clinic begins."

"No problem," replied the blacksmith. "I was getting carried away there."

"Come on, everyone," said Dr. Adam. He got the heap of jackets they'd piled onto a chair in the corner. "You should have enough information on pit ponies now to fill a whole book," he said to Mandy, handing over her coat.

Mandy nodded. "Just about. And James knows a whole lot more about tunnels now!" She grinned.

James winced briefly, then smiled back at Mandy. "I've seen enough to know that I don't want to go down another tunnel for a long time," he said.

At the door to the restaurant, Arthur said good-bye,

saying that he'd be sending a report on the incident to the Commission for Mine Safety. "They'll want to know every single detail. They might contact you if they need to check anything," he explained, then he set off down the hall toward his office.

"Wow," said James. "We're going to be in an official report!"

"Well, hello again." Mandy recognized at once the throaty voice behind them.

They all turned to see Mr. Newbury and Ceri from the Sunfield Pony Sanctuary.

"Lisa said you were here," said Mr. Newbury. Then he added grimly, "She told us about your narrow escape. I just can't believe what happened." He looked at his granddaughter. "It puts our problem in perspective, doesn't it?"

"What problem?" asked Dr. Adam.

"Just a financial one," said Mr. Newbury gloomily. "We're not breaking even with our accounts. I've cut as many corners as I can, but we're still not making enough money to support the sanctuary. If I can't find some way of staying afloat, we might have to close. But really, in the light of your narrow escape, it doesn't seem terribly important."

"Of course it's important," cried Mandy. Anything involving animals was always important!

"What would happen to the ponies if you did have to close?" asked James.

"Grandad would have to find new homes for them," explained Ceri sadly.

"That would be terrible!" gasped Mandy. The few hours she'd spent at Sunfield had been enough for her to see how happy and well looked after all the ponies were. She couldn't imagine that they would ever find better homes. On top of that, they'd all been through so much already. It wouldn't be right for the ponies to have to go through another upheaval.

"It could be our only choice," said Mr. Newbury. His weathered face looked more creased than ever. Mandy could see by his expression that his ponies meant the world to him. Despite what he'd said, he was obviously worried sick about his horses.

"Don't you have any other options?" asked Dr. Emily.

"I'm pinning all my hopes on registering Sunfield as a charity," Mr. Newbury replied. He went on to explain how he hoped to raise money by asking supporters to sponsor individual horses. They would be able to visit the sanctuary and adopt a pony. "And for people who live too far away to visit us, we're making a brochure showing pictures of all the horses. Then they can choose which pony they'd like to sponsor."

"What a fantastic idea!" exclaimed Mandy.

"Great!" agreed James.

"Do you really think so?" asked Mr. Newbury hopefully. Then he looked at Mandy. "And we're including a page or two on the pit ponies to try to create more interest in them."

Ceri held up a thick envelope she was carrying. "We borrowed these photos from the museum. Grandad wants people to be able to see pictures of the ponies working underground. We're even going to include the family histories of our pit ponies." She reached into the envelope and pulled out a few sheets of paper, which she showed to the group. On each sheet there was a diagram that showed each pony's family tree.

"This is really interesting," said James, looking at the family tree for Margot, the brown Shetland pony they'd met at the sanctuary. "How did you get all this information?"

"It was easy," Ceri answered, putting the papers back in the envelopes. "The museum still has the breeding and veterinary records of every pony that worked at Amberton. So we just had to search through them to find the records for our ponies at Sunfield."

"Well, it looks like there are going to be two projects about the Amberton pit ponies." Dr. Adam chuckled. "We must get going now. Good luck with the fundraising," he said, shaking Mr. Newbury's hand warmly.

"Send us a brochure when they're ready, won't you?" he added, before turning to leave.

"Wait, Dad," said Mandy desperately, as a shiver slowly made its way up her spine. "Could we look through the photos quickly? Please? I might find out something new for my project." This could be the last chance she'd have to discover who the mysterious pony was.

Dr. Adam looked at his watch. "We really need to be getting back to Animal Ark — but I suppose a few minutes won't make much difference."

Mr. Etherington took the bulky envelope from Ceri and began to take out the photographs. A few fell to the ground. Picking them up, the blacksmith suggested that it would be easier for Mandy to study the pictures properly if they were back on the wall alongside their accompanying captions in the gallery.

They followed Mr. Etherington out into the courtyard, passing the damp metal hulks of the mining machinery before pushing open the big wooden doors to the blacksmith's yard. The rain was now no more than a soft drizzle and the sky had grown lighter.

"Looks like the weather's clearing up," said Paul Newbury.

They climbed the short flight of stairs up to the gallery. Then, with Ceri passing the pictures to him, Mr.

Etherington began putting the photographs back in their places.

"I remember this fellow well." Mr. Etherington held up a picture of a white Shetland pony. "Steel, they called him. He was a tough one and smart, too. The rascal used to sneak mints out of my pockets. His handler told me that he could even open his flask and drink all the water from it. I didn't believe him until I saw it with my own eyes!"

While he replaced the photographs on the wall, Mr. Etherington told them what he could remember about each of the ponies. Mandy listened carefully, occasionally making notes on a small pad. It was wonderful to hear about the individual personalities of the ponies. It made her feel as if she knew them. They were no longer just a collection of photographs of unknown horses. But still, the nagging feeling persisted. Somewhere, there was an important clue that she was sure would resolve all her unanswered questions.

"Last one," said Ceri, putting down the envelope on a shelf next to the wall and handing the photograph to the blacksmith.

Mandy felt disappointed. It looked as if she wasn't going to learn anything new after all.

Mr. Etherington took the picture and hung it in the remaining gap on the wall before stepping aside. Mandy leaned forward to get a good look at the pony. What she saw sent a shiver down her spine. Here, at last, was what she'd been looking for all along!

"I know him," she gasped, taking a step closer. "It's the colt we saw in the tunnel!"

James looked over her shoulder. "It is," he echoed, his eyes wide with wonder.

A sturdy chestnut Shetland pony stared out at them from the photograph. His handsome face wore a proud, intelligent look. But it was his gaze that sent a wave of shock through Mandy. It was the same intense gaze she had felt in the tunnel. There was no doubt in her mind that this was the pony that had led them to safety.

Ten

"I *knew* we'd eventually find out who he was."

"*And* that he wasn't just a mirage!" said James pointedly.

"You saw *this* pony?" Ceri asked, exchanging a look of bewilderment with her grandfather.

"Yes," cried Mandy excitedly. "I'd know him anywhere. Wouldn't you, James?"

"Uh-huh," agreed James, still examining the picture. "You can't mistake the white star on his forehead," he said.

The others clustered around the photograph. After a few tense moments, Dr. Adam finally shook his head.

"Even if you two *did* see a pony in the mine — and I still think that's unlikely — it couldn't have been this one. Look at the dates under his picture — he died more than thirty years ago."

Mandy breathed in sharply. She stepped forward to read the dates. It was true. The colt had been dead for a long time. But she *couldn't* have been mistaken!

Mr. Etherington, who had been standing quietly to one side, began to speak. "It's all starting to make sense now," he said darkly, and Mandy experienced a shiver of anticipation.

"But nothing's making any sense!" Mr. Newbury was so confused that his face was more creased than ever. Mandy had to suppress a giggle at the way his friendly features seemed to disappear among his wrinkles.

Mr. Etherington began to explain. "I knew that pony well. He died a hero and became a legend. Even those who never knew him talk about his courage — even now." He pointed over the railing of the gallery toward the yard below. "We even have a memorial to him down there."

The blacksmith led them back down the stairs and across the yard to an area that Mandy and James had previously overlooked. The wet cobblestones glistened under the weak sun that had begun to shine down from the watery sky. Autumn leaves blew across the ground in the gentle, drying breeze that whispered through the yard.

Mr. Etherington gestured to the cart that was mounted on a block of concrete behind a chain-link fence. "The pony pulled a cart like this through the mine."

A monument bearing an engraved plaque stood in front of the fence. Mandy bent down to read the plaque. Her heart leaped as she read the first word. DEFENDER.

"*Defender,*" Mandy read aloud. "*In memory of a colt who went beyond the call of duty to save his master and, in so doing, lost his own life. His courage and loyalty knew no bounds. Those who knew him will never forget him.*"

A lump formed in Mandy's throat. She turned to Mr. Etherington. "You said you knew him. What happened? Why did he die?" she asked, her voice faltering.

Mr. Etherington swallowed hard. Mandy could see that the memory of the pony still saddened the man. "Just over thirty years ago, there was a serious earth-quake in the mine," he began. "Defender was on shift that day. His handler was a man who never really bonded with the ponies. He looked at them just as working machines. They'd been hauling coal up the tun-nel to the coal-removal shaft for about three hours and were on their way back for yet another load, when Defender suddenly stopped. The handler urged him on but the colt just stood his ground. He wouldn't budge an inch."

Mandy pictured the handsome little pony stubbornly refusing to move while the handler pulled and tugged at his harness.

"The handler began yelling at the poor creature to get a move on but Defender resisted him and stayed put. As he carried on, the colt suddenly started to whinny frantically." Mr. Etherington spoke softly, almost as if he was ashamed to talk about the brutal treatment of the colt.

Mandy had a flashback to the heartrending whinnying in her nightmares. In that instant, she knew without a doubt that the pony she'd dreamed of was Defender. And he *had* been trying to warn her of the cave-in. But there was no time now to ponder the strangeness of it all. Mr. Etherington was continuing with his story.

"The colt then started to move backward, pushing the cart back up the tunnel," he told them. "The handler had to turn and go farther up the tunnel, otherwise he'd have been injured by the heavy cart. He swore and yelled at Defender, but the pony just kept backing up. Then the cart jackknifed, blocking the pony's path. Defender couldn't go any farther — he was stuck."

Mandy held her breath as she pictured the terrible drama in the tunnel.

James, standing next to her, whispered, "I don't think I want to know the ending."

"Before the handler could straighten the cart," continued Mr. Etherington, "a sinister rumbling sound filled the tunnel. He realized then that they were in trouble. He tried to free Defender and grabbed at the cart, jerking and yanking at it with all his might. But it was too late. The roof of the tunnel suddenly caved in right above the colt. Moments later, Defender was buried under tons of rocks. And where they had stood, the tunnel was completely blocked."

There was not a sound in the yard as Mr. Etherington came to the end of his story. Mandy felt hot tears running down her cheeks. She brushed them aside, but fresh ones took their place. She bit her lip as she murmured quietly to James, "Defender lived up to his name. He protected his master. If he hadn't backed up, the man would also have been killed."

James sighed. "If only he'd understood what Defender was trying to tell him. Then the pony would have survived, too."

Mandy thought about the way the pony had warned her and James of the danger in the mine. It had been almost impossible to ignore him. How could the miner — who worked so closely with him — not have taken the young pony seriously? She shook her head sadly. The

colt had sacrificed himself for the sake of a cruel master. And even though he'd been mistreated, Defender
continued to help.

Mandy kicked at the cobblestones in anger. "He
shouldn't have died like that," she murmured. "His handler should have known!"

"I'm sure if it had been me, I would have taken him
seriously," muttered James.

"But you and Mandy did," Mr. Etherington said sin-

cerely. Mandy knew then that the blacksmith was the one adult who believed the colt had saved them, too.

She looked up as the yard was suddenly bathed in bright sunlight. At the same time, the curious vision of the closing eyes she'd had in the elevator earlier flashed through her mind. The real meaning of that image then dawned on her. Defender was now at peace! She could almost imagine him gazing contentedly. She looked at the cart that was shimmering in the sunshine and whispered, "Good-bye, Defender. And — thank you."

Dr. Emily ran a hand through her hair. "It's an extraordinary story," she said quietly.

"Amazing," agreed Dr. Adam. He looked at the somber group around him. "But I don't think we need to be so sullen. After all, it is a heartening story. And it just confirms how dependent we really are on our four-footed companions."

Dr. Adam's words seemed to cheer everyone up. Mandy glanced at her mom, who smiled back at her. "If a pony can save a life in that way," said Dr. Emily, "I can almost understand why people believe that horseshoes bring luck."

"Horseshoes! That reminds me," said Mandy. She turned to Mr. Etherington. "Do you always put Defender's name on your horseshoes?"

Mr. Etherington looked puzzled. "What do you mean?"

"You know! You carved 'Defender' on that miniature shoe you gave me," explained Mandy.

"No, I didn't," said the blacksmith. "I don't engrave anything on my horseshoes."

Mandy was puzzled. She knew she'd seen — and touched — the name on the horseshoe.

She waited for James to back her up, but he just looked back blankly at her. Obviously his shoe didn't have the colt's name on it.

She decided to drop the subject. Perhaps this time she *had* been mistaken. Still, she could have sworn she'd seen the name through the magnifying glass.

Dr. Adam jabbed her playfully in the ribs. "I think we've had enough mysteries for one day," he said, grinning. "And I also think that if we don't get a move-on now, we're going to be horribly late getting back to Animal Ark."

"Hey! That tickles, Dad." Mandy laughed and jumped out of his reach.

They walked across the yard toward the wooden doors. At the forge, Mr. Etherington stopped and, with a mock salute, said, "Well, good-bye."

Mandy and James hung back while the others went on. James shook the blacksmith's hand and thanked him for showing him how to make a horseshoe.

"I enjoyed it, too," he said.

"And thank you for telling us about Defender," said Mandy.

The blacksmith winked at her, picked up an iron poker, and began prodding the fire. A huge orange flame leaped up from the coals, casting a bright glow all around the forge.

The flame darted higher as it consumed the coals that cracked and fizzed beneath it. Mandy felt herself drawn to the fire. She couldn't take her eyes off it. The flame danced higher and gradually changed its shape. Mandy's heart skipped a beat. The flame almost looked like a glowing pony!

She shook her head and blinked and the flame resumed its normal shape. What could this mean? But before the question had even finished forming in her mind, she knew the answer. Flame! The pony at the sanctuary! There was just one last thing she needed to sort out.

Mandy spun around and dashed toward the gallery.

"Hey!" yelled James. "What's going on?"

"Come quickly, James," she yelled back. "I've just realized something very important." James charged after her, his boots hitting loudly on the cobblestones.

"Mandy! James!" called Dr. Emily, turning to see what the noise was about. "Where are you going?"

"Just a minute, Mom," Mandy shouted, taking the

stairs two by two with James at her heels. "I almost left something behind!" She ran to the shelf where Ceri had left the envelope. Picking it up, Mandy pushed her hand inside and felt for the papers she knew were still in there. The family trees — they held the answer. She pulled them out just as Ceri ran up the stairs and into the gallery.

"I wish you'd tell us what you're doing," said James, leaning against the wall and panting hard.

"Here," said Mandy, handing him and Ceri a few of the diagrams. "Look through those for Flame's family tree."

James stared at Mandy with raised eyebrows.

"Don't worry," she laughed. "I haven't gone crazy. You'll see."

They scanned the papers until Ceri waved one in the air. "Here it is," she announced. "Flame's family."

Mandy took the diagram from Ceri and, her heart pounding in her chest, read out the names. "Dan, Rosy, Sire . . ." She paused, then in a hushed voice read, *"Defender."*

At last, everything had fallen into place. She closed her eyes and pictured the little strawberry Shetland that had so forcefully claimed her attention at the sanctuary. "I should have known," she murmured. "He's got his father's eyes!"

*　　*　　*

The sun was pouring out of a cloudless blue sky as they drove back to Animal Ark. The hills and meadows sparkled in the bright sunlight and the air was fresh and clean, washed by the rain of the past few days. Mandy felt relaxed and happy.

Dr. Adam glanced at her in his rearview mirror. "Do you know, it's the first time in about a week that you've smiled?" he said.

"I know." Mandy grinned. "And I don't think I'll be having any more nightmares."

"What about your unfinished project — isn't that becoming a bit of a nightmare?" teased James.

"Don't remind me," moaned Mandy. "I think I'll be staying up all night working on it!"

"Talking about projects on pit ponies," began Dr. Emily. "I've been thinking." She twisted around in her seat and looked back at Mandy. "Why don't we all chip in and sponsor one of the Sunfield ponies?"

"Great idea, Mom!" exclaimed Mandy. "And I know already which one we should pick."

"I bet I know who that is," said James.

Mandy grinned at her friend. "Well, after everything that's happened, who else could we possibly choose but Flame?"

Look for the next spooky
Animal Ark ™ Hauntings title:

FOAL IN THE FOG

As Mandy followed the left bank of the Teign, the ground quickly became squelchy and soft underfoot. Mud sucked at Cinders's hooves, and from time to time the little mare stopped to nibble at a tuft of grass.

"No time for a snack," Mandy told her, pulling the pony's head up. She allowed Cinders to pick her own way, checking to make sure the river was on their right. Walking gingerly through the thickening mist, Cinders took her down a short slope and toward a clump of dark, shadowy trees. As they drew closer, the trunks loomed up through the mist, suddenly sharp in focus.

"I don't remember seeing these trees before," Mandy

said, her voice sounding loud in the mist-laden silence. She realized that she could no longer hear the familiar gurgling of the river water. Mandy drew Cinders to a halt and looked around her. She began to feel a little nervous. The gully was no longer beside them. "Go ahead, Cinders," she urged, nudging her with her heels. "Home!"

The pony walked on, but Mandy could tell she was hesitant. The mist pressed in on them, leaving Mandy's face damp and cold. She used her sleeve to wipe her cheeks and upper lip. Beyond the trees, she looked hopefully for a landmark — a house, a road, something. Drifting clouds had settled low across the moor, and, with a start, Mandy realized she had completely lost her sense of direction. Where had they parted from the Teign?

"Louise isn't far behind," she announced to the pony, trying to keep their spirits up. But the moor, so beautiful in the spring sunlight earlier that morning, now seemed a desolate place. It was colorless and chilly, and under the shadow of low clouds it almost felt unfriendly.

Mandy listened, hoping to hear the faint sound of Fern's approach or Louise's call. Nothing came. Even the birds were silent. Cinders slowed to a stop and sniffed the damp air. She shifted around, her ears twitching.

"Oh, no," said Mandy to the pony, finally facing the truth. They were lost. "What do we do now, girl?"

Cinders snorted and stamped her hoof. There was nothing to go on, no clue to tell them which way to go. The mist enveloped them completely. The moor seemed to have drifted away, leaving Mandy and her pony stranded in a sea of dense cloud. She sat still, holding the reins slack, trying to take comfort from the warmth of Cinders's flanks through her jodhpurs. There was no way of knowing how far they had strayed from the river, but she couldn't risk striking out deeper across the moor. The thought of plunging into one of the dreaded carpet bogs was enough to help Mandy make up her mind.

"We'll have to head back the way we've come," she announced to Cinders. "We need to try to find the river again."

Mandy peered at the ground for signs of Cinders's hoofprints as they walked along. They were easily visible in places but, in others, the soggy brown earth had swallowed up all traces. The few Mandy could see led her back to the clump of trees they had passed earlier, and her spirits rose. "We're not very far from the river now," she said aloud. Feeling happier, she opened her mouth to sing a song she'd learned recently for the school play, but she shut it again quickly. She'd heard a noise that, at first, she couldn't place. Mandy pulled Cinders to a halt and listened. It was the rumble of wheels on a road. She'd been listening for the sound of the river. The hum of a car's engine was the last thing she'd expected to hear. "It's a car!" she cried. "We must be near a road. If we hurry, we can ask them for directions."

She pressed her heels into the pony's sides and faced her in the direction of the noise. Cinders broke into a trot. Mandy aimed toward the sound. She and Cinders got to the top of a hill, where the mist was thinner. She could just make out a slope of butter-yellow gorse and a granite mound to the left. A ribbon of road snaked away in front of her. Turning her head from side to side, she looked for the car, but it was nowhere to be seen.

And then there was a terrifying squeal of brakes, lasting several seconds. Shock clutched at Mandy's heart. She hunched her shoulders and covered her ears.

The sound of metal being ripped apart came ringing across to her, along with the splintering crash of breaking glass. An acrid smell of burning rubber filled her nostrils.

"Oh, no!" Mandy gasped. The silence that followed

the crash was more frightening than anything else. She longed for footsteps, a shout, even a cry for help. She strained to see the accident. The mist seemed to have gotten thicker again, making it impossible to see anything. She gathered her courage and dismounted, reasoning that she would be more able to help on her feet.

"Wait for me, girl," she said. "I'll be back." She looped Cinders's reins around a branch of prickly gorse, her hands trembling with shock. It had sounded like a terrible crash. Would anyone be injured? Mandy gave Cinders a quick pat and set off down the slope toward the road.

As she ran, she stumbled over sharp stones, glossy green with moss, her arms outstretched against any unseen obstacles in the mist. "I'm coming! I'll help you," she shouted, reaching the road.

She looked around wildly, expecting to see the smoking wreck of a car, but the road was empty. Just ahead of her, the wraithlike mist suddenly thinned. Mandy gasped as a skewbald foal came hurtling through the curtain of fog, its short tail flying out behind it. The thud of its unshod hooves on the road seemed deafening in the quiet. Mandy's heart hammered as she looked into the face of the foal. It slid to a halt and stared at her for a moment, lifting its small white nose. Its eyes were wide, and its nostrils flared as its sides heaved. And then the foal spun away up the side of the bank and streaked across the moor, vanishing as quickly as it had appeared.

Mandy was rooted to the spot. Maybe the foal had been traveling in the vehicle she'd just heard crash!

Cinders's warm breath nuzzling her hand made her jump. The mare's reins must have come loose, and she had made her way down to the road to find Mandy.

She reached out to reassure her with a gentle stroke. "Come on, girl," she said gingerly, swinging up into the saddle. "We'd better take a closer look."

At Mandy's urging, Cinders set off up the road at a brisk trot. A breeze had sprung up, blowing the mist away. Mandy sensed that Cinders was happier now that the way ahead was clear. But there was still the scene of the accident to be found. Peering to each side, Mandy followed the road in one direction, then turned and headed back the other way. But there was no sign of a car — no tire marks scorched into the earth, no signs of the grassy shoulders of the road having been torn up by a vehicle veering out of control.

Strange, Mandy thought to herself. And what about the foal? What if it was injured? It had seemed okay, but it was definitely frightened. It could so easily get lost on the vast moor. Maybe she should try to find it. But it was dangerous, rushing off across an unknown stretch of moor that might be studded with carpet bogs.

Mandy slowed Cinders and caught her breath. She had to avoid getting lost a second time, now that she had managed to find the road. She needed to get home to organize a search party to find the car that had crashed.

"Which way?" Mandy asked Cinders. There was a rumble of thunder overhead. Cinders hesitated for a moment, then she turned right and set off at a brisk walk. "I hope you know where you're going this time," Mandy said, patting the pony.

At least the mist along the road was lifting, and as they made their way forward Mandy felt a little easier. There was a second roll of thunder, and the first drops of rain began to fall. She listened to the sound of Cinders's hooves striking the pavement in the silence and thought about Louise. Had she managed to get Fern to go across the narrow bridge? Perhaps she was already back at Whitehorse Farm, wondering what on earth had happened to Mandy and Cinders.

Just then, she heard the sound of an approaching car.